Dirty Wicked

Also from Shayla Black

Doms Of Her Life (by Shayla Black, Jenna Jacob, and Isabella LaPearl)
Raine Falling Collection (Complete)
One Dom To Love
The Young And The Submissive
The Bold and The Dominant
The Edge of Dominance
Coming Soon:
Heavenly Rising Collection
The Choice (Coming Fall 2017)

Stand Alone Titles
Naughty Little Secret
Watch Me
Dangerous Boys And Their Toy
"Her Fantasy Men" – Four Play Anthology
A Perfect Match

HISTORICAL ROMANCE (as Shelley Bradley)

The Lady And The Dragon
One Wicked Night
Strictly Seduction
Strictly Forbidden

Brothers in Arms
His Lady Bride, Brothers in Arms (Book 1)
His Stolen Bride, Brothers in Arms (Book 2)
His Rebel Bride, Brothers in Arms (Book 3)

PARANORMAL ROMANCE

The Doomsday Brethren
Tempt Me With Darkness
"Fated" (e-novella)
Seduce Me In Shadow
Possess Me At Midnight
"Mated" – Haunted By Your Touch Anthology
Entice Me At Twilight
Embrace Me At Dawn

Jen- Enjoy!

Dirty Wicked

A Wicked Lovers Novella

By Shayla Black

1001 Dark Nights

EVIL EYE
CONCEPTS

Dirty Wicked
A Wicked Lovers Novella

Copyright 2016 Shelley Bradley LLC
ISBN: 978-1-942299-57-8

Foreword: Copyright 2014 M. J. Rose

Published by Evil Eye Concepts, Incorporated

Sign up for the 1001 Dark Nights Newsletter
and be entered to win a Tiffany Key necklace.

There's a contest every month!

Go to www.1001DarkNights.com to subscribe.

As a bonus, all subscribers will receive a free
1001 Dark Nights story
The First Night
by Lexi Blake & M.J. Rose

Discover 1001 Dark Nights Collection One

FOREVER WICKED by Shayla Black
CRIMSON TWILIGHT by Heather Graham
CAPTURED IN SURRENDER by Liliana Hart
SILENT BITE: A SCANGUARDS WEDDING by Tina Folsom
DUNGEON GAMES by Lexi Blake
AZAGOTH by Larissa Ione
NEED YOU NOW by Lisa Renee Jones
SHOW ME, BABY by Cherise Sinclair
ROPED IN by Lorelei James
TEMPTED BY MIDNIGHT by Lara Adrian
THE FLAME by Christopher Rice
CARESS OF DARKNESS by Julie Kenner

Also from 1001 Dark Nights

TAME ME by J. Kenner

Discover 1001 Dark Nights Collection Two

WICKED WOLF by Carrie Ann Ryan
WHEN IRISH EYES ARE HAUNTING by Heather Graham
EASY WITH YOU by Kristen Proby
MASTER OF FREEDOM by Cherise Sinclair
CARESS OF PLEASURE by Julie Kenner
ADORED by Lexi Blake
HADES by Larissa Ione
RAVAGED by Elisabeth Naughton
DREAM OF YOU by Jennifer L. Armentrout
STRIPPED DOWN by Lorelei James
RAGE/KILLIAN by Alexandra Ivy/Laura Wright
DRAGON KING by Donna Grant
PURE WICKED by Shayla Black
HARD AS STEEL by Laura Kaye
STROKE OF MIDNIGHT by Lara Adrian
ALL HALLOWS EVE by Heather Graham
KISS THE FLAME by Christopher Rice
DARING HER LOVE by Melissa Foster
TEASED by Rebecca Zanetti
THE PROMISE OF SURRENDER by Liliana Hart

Also from 1001 Dark Nights

THE SURRENDER GATE By Christopher Rice
SERVICING THE TARGET By Cherise Sinclair

One Thousand and One Dark Nights

Once upon a time, in the future…

*I was a student fascinated with stories and learning.
I studied philosophy, poetry, history, the occult, and
the art and science of love and magic. I had a vast
library at my father's home and collected thousands
of volumes of fantastic tales.*

*I learned all about ancient races and bygone
times. About myths and legends and dreams of all
people through the millennium. And the more I read
the stronger my imagination grew until I discovered
that I was able to travel into the stories... to actually
become part of them.*

*I wish I could say that I listened to my teacher
and respected my gift, as I ought to have. If I had, I
would not be telling you this tale now.
But I was foolhardy and confused, showing off
with bravery.*

*One afternoon, curious about the myth of the
Arabian Nights, I traveled back to ancient Persia to
see for myself if it was true that every day Shahryar
(Persian: شهريار, "king") married a new virgin, and then
sent yesterday's wife to be beheaded. It was written
and I had read, that by the time he met Scheherazade,
the vizier's daughter, he'd killed one thousand
women.*

Something went wrong with my efforts. I arrived in the midst of the story and somehow exchanged places with Scheherazade – a phenomena that had never occurred before and that still to this day, I cannot explain.

Now I am trapped in that ancient past. I have taken on Scheherazade's life and the only way I can protect myself and stay alive is to do what she did to protect herself and stay alive.

Every night the King calls for me and listens as I spin tales. And when the evening ends and dawn breaks, I stop at a point that leaves him breathless and yearning for more. And so the King spares my life for one more day, so that he might hear the rest of my dark tale.

As soon as I finish a story... I begin a new one... like the one that you, dear reader, have before you now.

Chapter One

Lafayette, Louisiana

Nick Navarro had been out of prison exactly thirty-five hours. Long enough to get a good night's sleep, stock up on a few necessities, and visit his old friends, the Santiago brothers. Then he'd started putting his P.I. skills to good use, methodically searching for the woman he hadn't forgotten a single detail about during the fifteen months of his incarceration.

He intended to hunt down the bastards who had framed him and offed his childhood friend so he could repay them in spades.

Sasha Porter was the key.

At first glance, it looked as if she had disappeared off the face of the earth. She'd fled her house, quit her job, abandoned her car, maybe even changed her name. But his gut told him she was still alive. She had reasons to fight.

He would burn down the world until he found her.

Nick was forcing himself not to pace manically when his doorbell rang, sounding above the din of pounding rain. He zipped his gaze to the clock. Quarter 'til midnight. Obviously this wasn't a social call. Had his late buddy's enemy gotten wind of him shaking the trees for Sasha? Or had that corrupt son of a bitch just come back for another pound of flesh?

With every light in the living room on, Nick couldn't pretend he wasn't home. Besides, he refused to let this asshole think he was afraid. So he drew his weapon and jerked the door open, wearing a snarl.

Nick expected trouble, a gunfight, a battle for his life. Instead, Sasha Porter stood under his little portico, clinging near the door to avoid the deluge of November rain. Without a coat, she shivered. An exhausted little girl slept on her hip under a baby blanket, blond curls askew. A ragged duffel bag hung over her other arm. Rain had seeped through Sasha's tattered blouse. Water ran down her cheek, which was marred with an unmistakable bruise. Dark circles discolored the skin under her hazel eyes, now wide with fear as she stared at his SIG. Cursing, Nick scrambled to holster his weapon.

This wasn't the woman he remembered, and she wore the struggle for her survival all over her delicate face. The sight made Nick seethe, but he managed to blank his expression and open the door wider.

"Hi, Mr. Navarro, we met once about three years ago. You probably don't remember me..." She drifted off nervously.

He ached to show her how wrong she was. Instead, he scanned her body. She'd lost weight, lost curves. He'd fix that. But as she had the first time he laid eyes on her, she incited a roaring lust in his blood that electrified every muscle, pore, and nerve ending. He didn't just want this woman; having her felt necessary to his sanity. It didn't matter that her honey hair straggled out of half a ponytail or that she wasn't wearing a shred of makeup. Baggy jeans, plaid shirt...whatever. Sasha stood here in all her goodness. Despite everything she'd been through, radiance shone from her eyes. The brightest of angels tempting the devil himself.

Then he remembered she was his childhood friend's beloved widow. He killed his smile.

"Mike Porter was my husband." Her voice still shook. "You visited our house once. I'm—"

"Sasha," he assured, determined not to frighten her. "Come in."

* * * *

Blinking at Nick Navarro in surprise, Sasha inched inside his surprisingly posh house, hyperaware that she was dripping on his travertine floors. "You remember me?"

"I never forget a face." He shut and locked the door behind her.

Because he'd once been a private investigator? She stared but his unreadable expression cloaked his thoughts.

Her late husband had called Nick a great friend…and a very dangerous man. Mike had made her promise to come to Nick if she ever needed help. Sasha was having second thoughts now.

Merely dangerous men could be reasoned with. Even they had limits. Staring at the six-foot-three mountain of muscle who holstered a gun he clearly wasn't afraid to use, she feared no one could reason with Nick Navarro.

Dangerous seemed far too tame to describe him. It wasn't just the harsh shave of his black hair down to mere stubble or the glimpse of new ink flirting with the edge of his gray V-neck. The T-shirt pulled across his chest and bunched around his thick biceps as if it strained to contain him. It molded so closely to his abs that Sasha could see his six-pack. Dark jeans cupped his bulge and tore a disreputable snag down his thigh. His black leather boots belonged on a biker.

Sasha swallowed.

Like the first time she'd met him, the air around him pinged with life. And violence. His conviction for rape certainly didn't give her a warm fuzzy.

The closer he came on silent footsteps, the more wildly her heart beat. Every speech she'd rehearsed seemed silly now. God, would begging for his help even do any good?

Without it, she and her baby would probably be dead tomorrow, certainly within a week. She prayed Nick's hatred of their common enemy was enough to persuade him to help her. She hoped Nick Navarro had a good side she could appeal to.

But she wasn't counting on it.

When he reached for her, Sasha stiffened. If he noticed her reaction, he said nothing. He merely lifted the heavy duffel bag from her drooping shoulder and slid it to the ground.

"You look tired, hungry, and cold." His dark gaze drifted over Harper. "You can't carry your daughter all night."

His words surprised her. Why wasn't he demanding to know the reason she'd rung his doorbell so late? Or why she'd come at all?

She wished she had the luxury of telling him that she and her baby would be fine, like she'd been saying to people since Mike's murder. But she couldn't afford polite lies anymore. Nick Navarro was her very last hope.

God help her.

"I'll be fine. But Harper has been sick. If you have a blanket she could curl up with while we talk, I'd appreciate—"

As if on cue, the girl coughed, raspy and deep. Between one fit and the next, she drew rattling breaths into troubled lungs.

"She needs a bed, Sasha. I have four in this house. Pick one and put her down." When she hesitated, he towered above her, eyes narrowed. "She needs sleep and a doctor. You need help. That's why you came, isn't it?"

It took everything Sasha had to stand her ground and nod.

"Do you have any clean clothes in there for her?" He gestured to the duffel.

"No."

"I'll take care of it. The bedrooms are down the hall. When she's settled, come back and tell me what you're after."

Without another word, Nick turned his back, pulled out his cell phone, hit a few buttons, and paced out of the cavernous foyer. Who was he calling at dang near midnight? He hadn't reacted at all like she'd expected when she'd rung his doorbell. But she couldn't worry about him now. Harper needed her.

Sasha dragged herself out of the foyer and down the long hall, until she came to the first bedroom. Airy, with two twin beds—she could tell that much in the dark.

Flipping on the light, she saw two plain beige comforters with soft white sheets. Nothing frilly. But a real bed would be a blessing for her baby. It had been so long since she'd slept in one, and this looked like heaven.

Stopping, resting, indulging—Sasha couldn't for long if they wanted to live.

As she eased off Harper's clothes, the poor girl barely moved. Across the hall, Sasha found a powder bath and coaxed the little girl awake long enough to use the potty.

Naked except for Barbie underwear, Sasha tucked her daughter into bed. Harper sighed as her head hit the pillow and she fell back asleep. A fever heated the child's brow. For over a week, Harper had been ill. It was getting worse. But she had no money, almost no medicine left. She feared going to a hospital and filling out paperwork would be like drawing a map of their location for the lethal man chasing them.

Fighting tears of exhaustion and worry, she kissed her daughter's cherubic face, pushing the pale hair from her forehead, praying a good night's rest would help cure her.

"Is she asleep?" Nick asked in low tones.

Sasha turned at the unexpected sound of his voice. He filled the doorframe completely, looking as solid and as massive as the door he replaced. She shivered.

"Yes. Thank you."

"She'll have new clothes tomorrow morning, size three-T. Everything in the duffel is in the washer now. A pediatrician will be here at nine."

Again, he'd surprised her. Kindness? "I promise, we'll get out of your hair immediately after the doctor leaves. And I'll pay you back as soon as I'm able. I just came to see you about—"

Three electronic beeps resounding through the house startled her. Nick dragged his rough gaze down her body. At his inspection, Sasha shivered. She had no idea what he was thinking.

"Come with me." Without waiting for her response, he turned and left down the hall.

Sasha hesitated.

He paused without turning back. "You came to talk to me about something. I'll be in the kitchen."

Dread and anxiety settled in her stomach. But she had no choice. With a backward glance at her sleeping daughter, she followed.

At the end of the hall and to the left, she crossed the foyer again, then passed under an archway. A thoroughly modern kitchen awaited on the other side. Hardwood floors and concrete countertops gleamed under recessed lighting, as did the dark, contemporary cabinets. A stainless refrigerator stood in one corner, perfectly matching the oven and microwave, which beeped again.

"Bobby Flay, I'm not," he said, yanking open the microwave door and pulling out two pieces of pepperoni pizza. "Sit."

She couldn't remember the last time she'd had anything resembling a full belly, and this smelled scrumptious. Her stomach rumbled.

He set the slices in front of her, along with a napkin. "Eat."

Sasha frowned at the plate. Nick meant to feed her? "For me?"

"Yeah." He gave her a self-deprecating smile as he put a can of beer in front of her. "I only have necessities here right now. Sorry."

"Beer and pizza?"

"Damn straight."

His reply seemed so…typical guy. So unlike the violent rapist his trial had painted him to be. She hid her surprise behind her napkin. Just who was she dealing with?

"Look, I appreciate the bed, the medical attention for Harper, and the food—"

"I'm not listening to you until you've swallowed every last bite of that. Chow down."

Sasha didn't have to be told twice. She devoured the pizza, conscious of Nick watching her every move with dark, intent eyes. What the heck was he thinking when he looked at her that way?

If they'd been in a different situation, she would have been ridiculously attracted to him. He had a rugged face dusted with dark stubble and bold male features. His mouth was a wide slash of full lips that looked totally equipped to provide hours of sin. That, coupled with his air of mystery, screamed danger. Not that he'd be interested in her. She hardly possessed the centerfold beauty he'd once been used to, according to Mike. She was completely safe. In fact, the way she looked now, he wouldn't touch her, even if she were the last female on earth.

It didn't matter. Sasha had stopped caring about superficial stuff long ago. And however tempting he looked on the outside, Nick Navarro's blood was ice, according to his rape victim's testimony. Even at his trial, he'd never said a word in his defense, simply accepted his conviction with a blank stare.

Sasha again questioned the wisdom of putting herself in his path. If Mike hadn't been murdered, she would have been a suburban soccer mom—not homeless and broke and running for her life, sleeping with one eye open to make sure her daughter stayed safe. Not at the mercy of a man society labeled a violent offender. But he knew how to play hardball with the people who threatened her and Harper. He alone knew how to end this nightmare.

Damn it, if only she had some bargaining chip to offer him…

Once her plate was empty, he set it in the stainless steel sink. Cautiously, Sasha sipped her beer, observing his crisp, watchful movements.

"Thank you for the food. I was hungry," she admitted.

"Has your daughter eaten?"

Sasha nodded. "We stopped at a diner down the road a while ago."

"And you didn't eat."

He didn't ask; he knew.

Sasha paused. She didn't want to voice the truth, but lying to him seemed counterproductive when she wanted his help. "I didn't have enough money for both of us to eat."

"Then you walked here in the rain?"

"Yes."

"Carrying her?"

The edge of censure in his tone frustrated her. "I didn't have any other options."

At her confession, he sat back in his chair. "And now you're going to tell me why you're here and how you came to be in this state."

It was a command as much as a question. Sasha took a deep breath and tried to remember the words she'd rehearsed. "You probably don't recall, but when you visited Mike at our house, Harper was a newborn."

"I remember."

Did he really? "About a year later, Mike's behavior changed. He turned anxious, secretive. For months, I didn't know he'd fallen into dicey political waters at work. He never gave me details, but I gathered his difficulty had something to do with his boss, Walter Clifford, the Orleans Parish district attorney. Then I overheard Mike talking to you on the phone a few weeks before…" She didn't want to finish that sentence and relive her husband's death again. "He told you that Clifford was dirty."

"As sin. He's responsible for Mike's murder."

"I know. Apparently, the man suspects Mike left behind some evidence that proves his corruption. In the last fifteen months, I've tried to figure out where he might have hidden it, to no avail. But I knew my husband. If he'd been about to blow a whistle, he had solid proof."

"Meanwhile, Clifford has had thugs and hit men chasing you, right? He's told you to hand your evidence over or he's going to turn you into fish bait."

"Harper first." Her voice broke. "If I don't produce the proof three days after her murder, then me."

Something terrible flickered across Nick's face quickly, then it was gone. Sasha couldn't decipher the expression, but resisted the urge to back away from him.

"Why do you assume I'm any better than Clifford?"

Sasha's heart stopped. *Why had she?* "I—I just thought…"

"That since Mike was my childhood friend, I'd want vengeance for him? That I'd help you out of the goodness of my heart?" He shrugged. "C'mon, I knew Porter well. He told you to steer clear of me unless it was a dire emergency. But you assumed that since I'm a convicted rapist, I didn't have many boundaries to cross, and murder wouldn't bother me. How do you know I have a conscience at all? How do you know I can't be bought by the other side?"

Had she been so desperate, so sure Mike would have steered her in the right direction, that she'd rationalized the very real risks of coming here?

Yes, and obviously she'd been naïve. She had to leave now.

Darting to her feet, Sasha charged out of the kitchen and to the hall. Harper. She had to reach her little girl, pluck her out of bed, and escape—somehow—before Nick Navarro stopped her. Would he turn her over to the people wanting to kill her baby? Or did he have some nefarious plan of his own?

In seconds, she heard pounding footsteps hunting her from behind. *Oh, God. Oh, God!* He was going to catch her before she and Harper could escape.

Suddenly, he clamped hard fingers around her wrist and yanked her around to face him. She nearly tripped and fell. Nick stopped her by bracing her against the solid width of his chest.

Before he could get a tight grip on her, she started fighting, clawing and kicking, aiming for his genitals. He dodged her, clamping his thighs around hers and capturing both wrists in his hands.

Then he took her to the carpet in the narrow hallway and lowered himself on top of her.

Sasha fought him with every bit of her strength. She was nearly a foot shorter and a hundred pounds lighter, and he had gravity on his side. Panic clawed her. She couldn't breathe.

No!

She'd failed Harper. Her baby didn't deserve to die because her father hadn't been sneaky enough to sidestep criminals and her mother hadn't been worldly enough to escape them.

Sasha kept fighting long after Nick had her contained. She tried not to sob. Crying would do no good.

"Stop!" With strong arms and long legs, Nick clamped down harder, finally holding her immobile.

Panting, her breath quivering, Sasha looked up into his endless inky eyes. She expected to see laughter, triumph, anticipation.

She saw regret.

So he wasn't looking forward to killing her and Harper. She doubted that would stop him.

Sasha wasn't above begging, not if it would save Harper. "Please, she's just a baby…"

"Shh. You and your daughter are safe with me. And I won't let Clifford's hit men near you."

No words could have shocked her more. "How do I know you're telling the truth?"

"You don't, not any more than I know if you're telling me the truth about whatever evidence Mike may have found. But you want protection from Clifford's hit squad. I want revenge against the asshole. Looks like we have to trust each other."

Could she? What other option did she really have? In this case, the devil she didn't know had to be better than the one she did. At least she hoped.

Sasha gave him a shaky nod. "I need help. I can't run anymore. They're getting closer. Harper is sick…"

"And you're exhausted."

"I don't have any money to offer you…"

He hesitated. "That's not what I want."

Then what was he after?

Even as Sasha's mind raced, she became aware of the inferno of heat Nick put off. It sank through her damp clothes, under her skin. For the first time in weeks, she felt warm.

"Um…I could clean your house."

"That service comes with the rental."

"I'll do your laundry."

Nick shook his head. "I know how to use the washer and dryer just fine."

"I-I can cook…"

For a quick second, he looked as if that intrigued him, then he scowled. "Takeout works for me."

Now what? Besides housework, her only other talent lay in scrapbooking, and she seriously doubted he'd want a personalized album commemorating the time he'd spent in prison. But she had to give him something. Relying purely on his good favor would be too dangerous.

"Then what do you want in return for your help?"

Above her, he shifted, grimaced. Confusion buzzed through her brain…until she felt his erection, lengthening and hardening between her legs.

Sasha sucked in a breath. Even through her jeans and his, she could tell he was large. She hadn't had sex—or any contact with a man—since the night before Mike's murder, and her neglected body didn't fail to notice that he was all male. The mixture of fear and desire confused her, even as his scent hung musky in her nose, dizzying her head. His stare melted with heat, pouring over her like liquid seduction.

The truth—the price he intended to extract from her—was in his eyes.

"Me?" Sasha breathed.

He stilled for a moment, studying her. Then, as if he couldn't resist anymore, he notched against her, his erection now like steel. He nudged her right where it counted, against that bundle of nerves that sent a streak of heat racing up her belly and down her legs.

Sasha closed her eyes. She had to be insane. He was a convicted rapist. Mike had told her that while Nick was one of his best friends, he didn't trust the guy with women.

Her body was just responding to stress, to her long abstinence. How many times had she fantasized about finding some way—any way—to forget the mess of her life for a few stolen minutes? Too many to count. But the heat simmering in her veins now couldn't have anything to do with Nick Navarro himself.

"You're kidding." She shook her head. He must be.

"Do I feel like I'm kidding?"

Sasha swallowed against the uptick of her heartbeat. "Why?"

"I've been in prison for over a year. You have to ask?"

He thrust his hips against her again. Like before, he hit the perfect spot, the one that still hadn't recovered from his last nudge. Fresh heat zipped through her, more intense than before. An ache began to pulse between her legs.

What was wrong with her?

"I meant why me?" Sasha heard the quiver in her voice. "I'm sure you know women who are younger, who don't have stretch marks and a C-section scar. Who—"

"I know a dozen Barbie dolls I could call now if I just wanted to fuck. You're real." He unclamped one of his hands from her wrist…then glided onto her breast. "This is real."

He sank his fingers into her giving flesh, dragging his thumb over her nipple. Sasha sucked in a breath. Despite her damp shirt and bra, she felt his touch all the way to her toes. Tingles skittered through her system. Her nipples puckered, beaded. Under his broad palm, he teased one of the buds with another slow caress. His rough breath rent the silence between them. She shut her eyes—and bit back a moan.

She had to be totally out of her mind. Why wasn't she fighting, screaming her lack of consent?

Her brain told her she'd lose any chance of persuading him to protect her and Harper. Loneliness reminded her how badly she'd missed human comfort. Her touch-starved body shouted the fact that there was something about Nick Navarro that lit up the long-suppressed woman inside her that had fantasized about silken satisfaction with a very capable man.

She was still trying to comprehend the moment—the caress of his talented fingers—when he dipped his head to torment the tight bud of her nipple through the fabric separating them. A pull. A nip. Pleasure seized her. Shivers racked her. So sudden. So shocking.

It terrified her.

"I won't be forced." Her voice sounded shaky, splintered.

Above her, Nick tensed and raised a brow. They both knew her body wanted him. Heat rushed through her veins, up her cheeks. But she made herself meet his stare. What was he thinking? What would he do? Had she just made a dreadful mistake?

Slowly, he withdrew his hand, then pushed himself away from her. He sat against the wall. Sasha felt the withdrawal of his heat instantly. Cold seeped into her body again, her damp shirt making her tremble. The guarded, slightly mocking expression on his face wasn't helping her nerves, either.

"I've never raped anyone in my life, including Fiona Normand."

Sasha backed away to the other wall and drew her knees into her chest. She almost thanked him for lying to her. His false words were a slap of reality, erasing the quick rise of her desire and her loss of sanity.

"You don't have to deny what happened. I read the testimony. I merely wanted you to understand—"

"I'm not denying a damn thing," he growled. "I'm telling you flat out that I didn't rape her. You need to know that. I don't want you fighting once I have you naked and under me."

He sounded awfully sure of himself. *Of course he is, idiot. He stands between your daughter and death. He's got you and he knows it.*

Sasha didn't see any way to avoid becoming his lover. She'd do anything to keep her baby alive.

"The expert testimony of the doctors at your trial found your skin under her nails and your semen in her…"

"I never denied fucking her, but I didn't force her to do anything she wasn't willing to do with me and hadn't done before."

A million thoughts spun through her head. Her stomach tightened. "It doesn't matter."

"It does. And I'm telling you the truth."

"Why would Fiona Normand lie?"

He shrugged. "The town princess told the policemen that the bad man lured her into opening her front door, then he raped her. How else was she going to explain being tied to her bed? Certainly not by admitting that she begged someone like me to bind her to it. It's all smoke and mirrors to prevent me from investigating her uncle, the very crooked Mr. Clifford."

Sasha felt her eyes widen. "Fiona is his niece?"

"Through marriage, but notice how the press didn't mention that? You can thank the cops and reporters he has stashed in his back pocket for neglecting to include that info."

The press didn't surprise her so much but… "Clifford is bribing the police?"

"You look shocked to find out the good guys can be bought." He smirked. "Yeah, he's paid them to disregard his shit for years."

"So…" She grappled to comprehend the depth of seedy corruption. "Fiona lied about everything that happened between you to protect her uncle? Why? I'd never protect anyone doing such awful things."

"If she let her Uncle Walter go down, where would her meal ticket be? So Fiona told him I was pumping her for information about Mike's disappearance." Nick smiled grimly. "Clifford set up the rest. Crying rape served the added bonus of preserving Fiona's precious reputation. She wasn't willingly having sex with a P.I. who had a record. No, I forced her." He cut her a mocking glare. "Of course."

Sasha wasn't sure what to believe. "How did you meet her?"

"I heard she and Clifford were close, so I picked her up in a bar. I suspected she knew all the dirty dealings her uncle was up to. I gave her whatever she wanted so she'd talk."

Even sex?

"Oh, my…" Sasha sat stunned. Nick had tried to work Fiona over, and in the end she'd worked him?

"I should have seen the con coming. I won't be played again." Self-recrimination filled his bitter tone. "Look, I never said I was a Boy Scout. I only said I didn't rape her."

Did she dare believe that or did she simply want to because she couldn't stomach the thought of giving her body to the kind of man who would hold a woman down and force his way inside her?

It didn't matter. It was felicity for her that Nick had been released from prison early for good behavior. Without him, she and Harper might be dead soon.

She drew in a deep breath. "You want sex in exchange for your help and protection. I understand. What are your exact terms?"

"Four weeks. It will take me that long to figure out how to play this, whether I should fake your deaths, find or fabricate evidence to discredit Clifford, or just kill the son of a bitch."

Kill? Her conscience balked. Logic reminded her quickly that the Orleans Parish DA had no such qualms about murder. He'd threatened to smother the life from her daughter. High-minded morals wouldn't keep her and Harper alive.

"Sasha." He snapped, bringing her attention back to him. "Hear me well. In those four weeks, the word 'no' never falls from your lips. Whatever I want, whatever I ask, you comply."

"You mean if you want us to hide at three in the morning, we do it? That's okay. We've been doing that for…it seems like forever."

"I mean that, too. But I'm also telling you that I expect perfect willingness in bed."

Shock knocked the air from her lungs. "You'd want someone giving you whatever just because you commanded it?"

"The commands are for your psyche, sweetheart. That way, you can tell yourself that you didn't have a choice, that of course you didn't like bedding down with a rapist. But honestly, I'm not going to do a damn thing to you until your body is good and wet and ready."

She digested his words in a panic and shook her head. "That may never happen."

His jaw tightened. "If I can't get you hot, I don't have any business between your legs. If you can't let go because you're afraid I'll hurt you, I'll persuade your body otherwise. That's a promise."

How was she supposed to respond to that? "Um, I'm sure you're perfectly capable of...arousing a woman. I meant that I may disappoint you if you're expecting some vixen. I—I'm not very sexual."

Nick stilled, then a smile quirked up the side of his mouth. "You will be."

Those words filled her with part dread—and if she was honest—part anticipation. Always, she'd been the good girl. She'd been a virgin on her wedding night, done her best to be a lady, even in the bedroom. Somehow, she didn't think Nick would appreciate her circumspect nature or accept her lying back and sorting through her mental to-do list during sex.

Then again, what choice did she have? Faking a few moans would be much easier than actually orgasming with a virtual—and very dangerous—stranger.

Sasha thought back to his touch on her breast, the way he'd rocked his hips against her. She'd felt something, far more than she expected. Maybe it would be enough to see her through.

"I—I'll do my best not to disappoint you," she murmured finally.

A laugh played across Nick's wide mouth. "Don't worry. I plan to be thoroughly satisfied."

She bit her lip, feeling a violent flush rush up her cheeks. Then silence ensued. What was left to say? For the next four weeks, she'd agreed to whore herself to a ruthless criminal fresh from prison. She had a full belly, her daughter was tucked safely into a bed, and a doctor would see Harper in the morning. Sasha really had no excuse to delay the inevitable.

She stood. Nick did the same. Their stares met. She ignored the jolt of awareness pinging through her body. Instead, she reached for her blouse, unbuttoned it, and slid it off her shoulders before dropping it on the floor.

Nick watched, nothing on his face giving away his thoughts. His gaze flicked over her shoulders, her breasts covered by a utilitarian white bra. Was he totally underwhelmed? Lowering her gaze, she saw he had a reaction to the fact she was nearly topless. He was undeniably hard, his bulge trying to burst through his jeans.

What was she supposed to do now? But she knew. She'd read books, watched a porn movie at a bachelorette party once, listened to Mike go on and on. Sasha knew what all men wanted.

Uncertainty quaking in her belly, she closed the distance between them and stopped in front of Nick. Then she dropped to her knees.

Chapter Two

Nick smothered a curse and clenched his fists. Sasha Porter was in front of him. On her knees. Looking up at him with big hazel eyes that said she'd do anything to please him.

The fantasy of her oral adoration had been a favorite he'd cha-chinged from his spank bank repeatedly for nearly three years. He was more than a little tempted to unzip and let her go to town.

She reached for his fly. He grabbed her wrists in a harsh grip. His breath sawed in the silence between them.

Nothing about her demeanor screamed horny, but Nick knew females. When he'd had her underneath him, her body hadn't been immune. Still, he couldn't let that fact fuck with his head. Taking Sasha up on the offer he'd coerced from her would make him a terrible bastard. Well, more terrible than he was. Despite his conviction, he'd never violate a woman who wasn't willing in every way.

"Nick?" she breathed. "Don't you want me to...?"

Suck his cock? *Fuck, yes.* "When I say so."

As she sat back on her heels, he stared. Who was this woman? Mike had called her modest, sexually restrained. In retrospect, Nick could see how months on the run had turned his buddy's prim wife into a pragmatist willing to give him a blow job to keep her kid alive.

And didn't he feel like a prick? Ten minutes ago, propositioning Sasha had seemed like the perfect antidote for his compulsion to touch her. If he spewed toxic bullshit that made her fear and loathe him, she'd stay far, far away. Then...boom. Temptation removed. Problem solved.

But here she knelt, blinking at him, pink lips softly parted. Blood surged to his cock until he swore his zipper would strangle it.

How's that plan working out for you now?

Mike Porter had been a true-blue kind of guy. A good friend. Undoubtedly, a model husband. He'd definitely been a protective one. If Mike could have read the thoughts running through Nick's head, his old pal would have wanted to castrate him. Unfortunately, neither that nor his guilt was stopping the endless loop of high-quality porn—starring Sasha—from playing in his head.

He had to get her the hell away from him.

"Hands down," he barked as he released her.

She complied, still staring at him in question. Though she tried to hide it, he couldn't miss the relief on her face. She was grateful for the reprieve.

"I'm sorry if I…" She bowed her head as if she wasn't sure what to apologize for and searched for something that wouldn't piss him off. Or maybe she couldn't stand to look at him.

He had no right to, but Nick thrust his hand around her ponytail and tugged just enough to force her gaze to him again. Visually was the only way he should touch her, but he threaded his fingers through her strands. Her hair slid like silk against his skin. "For what, rushing me? Crowding me?"

"Yes."

Liar. A grim smile danced at the corner of his lips. She apologized so he wouldn't change his mind about helping her and protecting Harper. Because she was afraid of him.

God, that made him feel low.

He released her, stepped away. "Take a shower. Get in bed."

"Y-yours?"

He'd fucking love that. The thought of unraveling her reserve and making her cling to him went straight to his dick.

"Stay with your daughter tonight. I'd rather have you once you've rested. Because once I start fucking you…well, expect a long night," he warned.

As he suspected, she shot to her feet and backed away from him. She could barely keep her opinion of him off her face. Yeah, he was a vile asshole. *Perfect.*

"I'll, um, leave you until morning." Her back hugged the wall as she edged away.

Nick grabbed her arm. "Wait." He brushed past her and grabbed a clean towel, a bottle of shampoo, and his comb from the master bathroom. He returned and put the items in her hands. "You'll need these. Sorry. That's the only comb I've got."

She frowned, looking utterly confused by his consideration. "Thank you."

"Rest. Let me know if you need anything."

"I will."

Another lie. If Sasha could afford to, she would walk away from him now. She'd certainly never ask him for anything else, believing every favor came with a price. The sooner they found Mike's evidence, the better for both of them.

He just hoped that breakthrough came before desire crushed his self-control.

* * * *

Harder than ever, Nick woke to a half-empty king-size bed. The morning would have been a whole lot better if Sasha Porter had been naked and sated beside him.

With a sigh, he glanced at the clock. Shit. Twenty past eight in the morning.

Hopping into a pair of sweatpants he'd discarded at the foot of the bed, he rushed down the hall to the first of the spare bedrooms. Why the hell Xander and Javier had rented him a huge house rather than just a crappy apartment near his old stomping grounds, he had no idea. He'd bet London had a hand in it. He had a soft spot for the woman who had helped to save his friends from self-destruction. He'd bet she had one for him for roughly the same reason.

The vague smile widened when he found Sasha wrapped up with Harper in one twin bed, sound asleep. A nearly empty bottle of children's Tylenol rested on the nightstand. Neither one looked as if sleep had helped much. Nick felt guilty that he hadn't realized Sasha might need a hand with her daughter. Hell, he had no experience with kids.

He walked into the enormous shower. Fantasizing about having Sasha under the spray, clinging to him and panting his name in his ear as she rose to climax was definitely more exciting than soaping up with a bar of Irish Spring. He didn't punch his express ticket to self-pleasure this morning. With Sasha under his roof, the idea fucking bored him. Instead, he cut the water, dried off, and made his way into a pair of jeans. His black T-shirt had a cartoon depicting terrified people fleeing a hulking figure pursuing from behind. The caption beneath read *ZOMBIES HATE FAST FOOD*.

Fingercombing his hair, he headed for the kitchen. When he reached the end of the hall, the doorbell rang. A glance out the window at the sleek Infiniti SUV told him exactly who stood on the other side of the door.

With a wry shake of his head, he opened up.

"Where is she?" London asked, her sweet face curious as she held her infant daughter and tried to peek around him.

"You forgot to say hello, *belleza*." Xander's smile revealed how much he adored his wife.

Javier didn't look any less smitten. "She's been pacing since she took Dulce out of her crib at six a.m. You're lucky we got her to wait this long before we headed over."

Nick opened the door wide and directed everyone to the kitchen. "Sasha and Harper are still asleep. Coffee?"

London walked in and gave him a loose hug around the neck. "Which I assume you want me to make?"

"Please," Xander all but begged. "Nick makes terrible coffee."

"It's a single-cup brewer, asshole," Nick shot back. "Foolproof."

"And yet you fucked it up yesterday morning."

Javier barked out a laugh as he carried in a couple of sacks of groceries. "You're both helpless." He plucked their seven-month-old out of London's arms and handed her to Xander. "Hold Dulce."

After Javier planted a kiss on the baby's head, he disappeared into the kitchen with London and tucked items into the refrigerator or pantry. Nick lingered with Xander in the adjoining dining room. It looked so weird to see the former manwhore holding a little girl in a frilly dress. With her daddies' dark hair and her mother's bright blue eyes, Dulce was going to be a beauty.

"Bought a baseball bat to fight off the boys yet?" he asked Xander.

"Screw some stick of wood. Guns are where it's at. I'm collecting an arsenal. Not one of those adolescent pricks is touching my daughter."

Spoken like an overprotective father. "What about when her teenage hormones kick in? She might want—"

"If you'd like our help, shut your fucking mouth."

Nick laughed. Yanking Xander's chain had always been on the fun side, but now it was a downright blast. "Shutting it now."

"Good man." Xander glanced across the kitchen to see Javier pulling London close before he dipped his head to cover their wife's mouth. Nick had seen them kiss before. Usually, they oozed passion; they still did. Both brothers had always looked at her as if she was their moon, sun, and stars. Their very happiness, in fact. But it was different now that they'd had a child. More reverent. More devoted. More sacred. They were a family in every sense.

Nick looked away and shoved aside a weird stab of envy he could totally do without.

"So what's your plan?" Xander asked, bouncing his daughter in his arms and smiling when she giggled.

"Like I said last night on the phone, I think the little girl is too sick to be anything but a distraction to Sasha. We should be focused on keeping her and her daughter safe. And if we wait for Harper to recover first...I think the kid having a cold will be the least of our troubles."

"Yeah. Given the contacts and resources Clifford has, he'll find you fast. I think you're right; Harper is better off with us and away from the danger."

Nick nodded. "Convincing Sasha will be the hard part."

"If she's half as attached to her daughter as London is to ours? Oh, yeah. She'll fight you like hell."

"I'm betting on it. But the solution to this shitstorm isn't going to magically roll up to my door. Sasha and I will have to search Mike's old stomping grounds for whatever he left behind. A sick kid is a liability. If she and I find what we're looking for, they'll have a chance to live happy, healthy lives."

"And the bastard who put you in prison will go down."

"That, too." Nick nodded.

"Then what? Got any plans beyond that? You haven't talked about reopening your business or taking on new cases." Xander looked at him as if he saw too much.

"I haven't thought that far ahead," he hedged. Who the hell would hire him now?

Xander raised a dark brow. "We'll make you head of security at S.I. Industries."

And fire the guy already occupying that position to create a vacancy for their ex-con pal? They had already done too much for him.

"Thanks, but you know I'm not much of a corporate guy. This is fancy office attire for me." He gestured to his T-shirt.

Xander rolled his eyes. "Because you never tried. Look, you've had some tough breaks, and I know you're probably thinking this is a pity hiring, but it isn't. Just…think about it."

"Nick?"

The sound of Sasha's startled voice saved him from answering Xander right away. He pushed away from the table and approached Sasha, who held Harper, coughing with red-cheeked abandon. "Morning."

She braced a hand on her daughter's back and cut a glance at Xander, who closed in behind him. He heard London and Javier approach, too.

Nick didn't follow Sasha's gaze. He couldn't take his eyes off her. Her clean hair looked rumpled and sexy in a pale cloud around her shoulders. Her hazel eyes were wide and wary. Then she looked to him instinctively for reassurance and safety. He felt a jolt of satisfaction—and the rise of his dick.

As he reached her, he couldn't stop himself from curling his hand around her shoulder and bracing his finger under her chin until she lifted her gaze to look at him. "These are my friends. They're here to help."

"You're sure they can be trusted?" she whispered.

Nick wasn't insulted. She'd probably stayed alive this long by questioning everything and everyone in her life. "Positive."

He forced himself to tear his gaze off her long enough to perform the introductions. London had backed away and now held Dulce so the baby wasn't exposed to any of Harper's germs. But she smiled and waved at Sasha with a warm friendliness that had Sasha almost smiling back.

"We brought groceries," London said. "If one of my husbands will hold the baby…"

Javier turned to pluck Dulce from her arms. "Go ahead. I'm sure Sasha and Harper would like a home-cooked breakfast. I know I would."

"Great. Maybe you'd like to talk to me while I get everything ready?" London asked Sasha. "We'll send the men to the living room. I'm sure they can find some college football pregame to watch until the doctor comes."

"Sure." Sasha didn't look as certain as her answer sounded, but she followed London into the kitchen, still carrying a limp, hot-cheeked

Harper.

Reluctantly, Nick followed the Santiago brothers into the living room as the sounds of bowls clacking and the gas stove firing filled the air. Female chatter followed.

"Let London work her magic. She's a warm, comforting presence," Javier murmured.

Yeah, Nick had liked her immediately back in the day and known she'd be good for the overly driven executive. The fact that she'd also settled the younger Santiago had been nothing short of a miracle.

"Everyone loves London," Xander assured.

"I just don't want Sasha to feel abandoned. She's out of her element as it is."

"She'll be fine." Javier dragged him to the sofa.

The moment he was seated, Xander plopped into a chair, leaned closer, and leveled a direct gaze at him. "You, I'm not so sure about, my friend."

"What do you mean?" Nick scowled.

"Why didn't you level with us? This isn't just about revenge, and don't try to bullshit us otherwise."

"I don't know what you mean," Nick insisted.

"This is also about Sasha," Javier insisted. "That's obvious to me now."

Fuck. They knew him too well. "Mike and I grew up together. If the shoe was on the other foot, he would have helped my wife out of trouble, too. I owe him. Before he died, he asked me to look into Clifford. I didn't get the goods; I just got set up. That bastard found the perfect means to get me out of the way so he could off Mike."

And if Nick hadn't failed, maybe the kid who had single-handedly pulled him out of the gutter would still be alive and raising the daughter he'd had with the wife he loved. Neither of them had imagined Clifford would have the balls to use his own niece to fabricate charges against Nick. They'd underestimated the bastard—and paid a terrible price.

"Right, but this is about more than helping your late buddy's widow," Javier pointed out. "You want her."

"You look at her the way my brother looks at our wife," Xander added. "The way I'm sure I look at London, too."

Desperate. Smitten. Hungry.

Fuck, what did he have to offer a woman? A bankrupt business? A prison record? Zero experience in making a monogamous relationship work? Life had already dealt her a tough hand. She deserved better, especially since Mike had been taken from her for good.

"Leave it," he told the brothers. "She doesn't want me and never will. I've made sure of it."

Javier clenched his jaw, a sure sign his legendary temper was brewing. "What did you do, you stupid bastard? Now isn't the time to be noble."

Certainly that's the last thing Sasha would call him. "I don't need romantic advice. I just need to keep her alive and solve her problem."

"We figured you'd say that." Xander sighed. "So we left a new SUV registered to S.I. Industries in our parking garage for you." He tossed the keys, and Nick caught them in his fist. "It should be clean. The gas tank is full. There's five grand in cash in the glove box."

"I'll pay you back."

"Shut up." Xander rolled his eyes.

"Know where you're going yet?" Javier asked.

"No. Sasha was too tired and worried about Harper last night for me to grill her with questions."

Today, Nick knew he couldn't afford to be so polite.

Javier pulled a device from his suit coat and slapped it in Nick's palm. "Here's a burner phone. Keep us posted. And we're serious about that job offer. When this is over… That's how you can pay me back."

"I appreciate it, man." He tried not to let gratitude choke him up. "I do, but…"

Xander cursed. "If you change your mind, the door is always open."

With a tense nod, Nick reached for the remote and flipped on the TV to see a group of suits reliving their former football glory days by drawing Xs and Os on a whiteboard and blustering at one another about the college squads scheduled to compete.

A few minutes later, London poked her head into the family room. "Food's on, boys."

"God, I love that woman," Javier professed as he rose, sniffing at something savory.

The smell made Nick's mouth water, too. Damn, he'd missed country sausage and gravy.

He and Xander followed Javier into the breakfast nook. They all took their seats around the table, Dulce bouncing on Javier's knee and sticking her little tongue out for some baby oatmeal London had fixed. Everyone else dug in to the hearty heaps of eggs, potatoes, and the amazing sage-rich sausage—except Sasha. She picked, far more concerned with trying to feed Harper than herself.

London finished a helping of eggs and some Greek yogurt, then pushed her plate away. "Sasha, why don't you let me try to coax Harper to eat?"

"We're fine. Finish your breakfast."

The woman was so stubborn it made Nick want to grit his teeth.

"I'm done," London insisted, wrinkling her nose. "I've still got a few pounds of baby weight to lose, and even though I'm not pregnant anymore, I still can't eat breakfast with the kind of gusto I used to."

At her grimace, Sasha looked down at Harper. The girl's eyes were half open, her cheeks red as she shifted listlessly.

"If it upsets her, I'll bring her right back. But no offense, honey"—sympathy filled London's face—"you look like you could use a decent meal."

Nick watched their conversation, more than a bit surprised when Sasha slanted her gaze his way. She wasn't looking for permission, but she sought his reassurance. *Interesting...*

He bent close to the little girl. "Harper?"

The child blinked her big green eyes up at him. God, she had so many of Mike's features that looking at her hurt.

The girl didn't speak but he had her attention. "Would you like to meet my friend?"

London waved at the girl. "Hi, Harper. I have a pink donut with sprinkles on it just for you..."

That made the little girl smile. She wriggled on Sasha's lap, seeking a way down. Nick plucked her up and walked her around the table to London. Harper went to the woman right away, looking up at her with unabashed curiosity as she brushed a honey-colored curl from her wary eyes with little fingers.

"Hi, pretty girl. I'm London," she cooed. "I'm guessing you like donuts."

Harper nodded. "Yesth."

She had the cutest lisp, and it tugged at something in Nick's chest.

"Can you get me the white bag on the counter?" London pointed vaguely.

"Sure." Nick plucked the bag from the gray slab next to the stove.

"Find the pink donut inside. And how about a plate?"

Nick fished out the pastry in question, then retrieved a dessert plate for the kid, whose eyes lit up like it was Christmas morning. When he set it on the plate, Harper grabbed it.

Xander and Javier laughed. Sasha sent her daughter a fond smile so sad, it nearly ripped out his guts. She was questioning every decision she'd made as a mother, despite the fact that she'd had so few choices.

"Why don't you break it into sections for her?" London asked him. "Then Harper will be ready to eat." She peeked around to the girl's face. "Won't you?"

"Pleath." Harper bounced on her lap.

Nick broke the pastry into four manageable pieces and set all but one on the plate. The last he handed to the girl, who grabbed it with a smile before she shoved it into her mouth with a noisy smack.

Everyone laughed again. She really was a cute kid.

As Harper settled in with her donut, London added a few eggs and potatoes to the plate. With a combination of jokes, smiles, and silly faces, London persuaded the girl to eat roughly half the food.

The doorbell rang. Nick whipped out his phone. Two minutes until nine.

"The doctor?" Sasha asked.

"Should be. Stay here." He rose and headed out of the kitchen.

Once he'd cleared Harper's line of sight, he unholstered his gun, keeping it tucked against his side as he cautiously opened the door. He made a mental note to ask Xander why the hell the place didn't have a damn peephole.

On the other side, he found a young female. The Asian woman looked petite and intelligent and not at all put off by his demeanor. "Mr. Navarro?"

"Dr. Minn?" At her nod, he holstered his weapon and threw the door wide. "Come in."

"Where's Harper?"

"Finishing breakfast."

He led the doctor to the kitchen. She hugged London and brushed a fond caress on the top of baby Dulce's head, then turned her attention to Harper. After a glance she frowned and looked across the table to Sasha. "Can you bring her to one of the bedrooms so I can examine her?"

Sasha rose, plucked her daughter from London's lap with a

whispered thanks, then disappeared down the hall. Nick stood awkwardly and watched them go. He wanted to know what was happening, had the most irrational need to stay beside Sasha. But Harper wasn't his daughter. Her medical condition wasn't any of his business.

London nudged his shoulder with her own. "Follow her."

"She wouldn't appreciate my intrusion." Nick already knew Sasha was a deeply private person.

"You're too smart to act this stupid. She's afraid and she needs a shoulder to lean on."

Like she'd ever allow the man who'd ordered her to put out to comfort her? "I'm sure she'd rather have a calming female presence."

Before he finished speaking, London shook her head. "Sasha feels like her sky is falling. She needs a pillar to keep the roof over her head."

Another woman couldn't do that for her?

London sighed as if she was losing patience. "She needs someone stoic who won't bend under pressure. She needs someone she perceives as stronger than her to rely on."

"But she's already strong. Given how underhanded and relentless Walter Clifford is, the fact that she's kept herself and Harper alive since Mike's murder is pretty much a miracle."

"But it's been a struggle. Can't you see that?"

Hard to miss. He nodded.

"I can guarantee that, at times, she's felt both very afraid and very alone. At the risk of sounding hopelessly unfeminist, she needs a man." London shook her head. "She needs *you*."

Nick doubted he could be what she needed but he owed Mike. He owed Sasha, too. "I'll take care of her."

Letting out a nervous breath, he made his way down the hall and paused in the threshold of the bedroom. The doctor had her stethoscope pressed to Harper's back as the child took rattled breaths. Sasha watched with worried eyes and a taut mouth.

Dr. Minn plucked the device from her ears and hung it around the back of her neck. "If I could X-ray her properly, I could tell you with absolute certainty what ails your daughter. Since that's not possible, I'm going to say that given her high fever, wheezing, and productive cough, she has pneumonia."

The air left Sasha's body as she froze, stood unmoving, not even to draw her next breath.

Holy shit. Harper's condition was far more serious than he'd imagined. Nick was damn glad Sasha had come to him when she had.

"Since it took her about four days to develop, it sounds viral, rather than bacterial, so giving her antibiotics won't do any good," the doctor went on. "But I don't like the way your daughter is breathing. If you won't admit her to the hospital, which is where she should be, she needs to stay home and rest a great deal, drink a lot of fluids, eat frequent but small meals, and be on oxygen."

"That's not possible." Sasha's voice trembled.

"Then I can't guarantee your daughter will recover." The doctor sounded clipped and disapproving.

The pediatrician didn't know Sasha's situation, so she couldn't possibly understand the woman's quandary. Still, Nick wanted to slap her and tell her not to judge.

Instead, he focused on Sasha. Worry stamped itself all over her face. How would Harper ever get that kind of rest and care when their very survival depended on them relocating ASAP—and probably more than once? He could actually see her weighing the probability that Harper would die if they stayed on the run versus the likelihood Clifford would slaughter them all if they risked calling a place home even temporarily.

In that instant, he saw what London meant. Sasha had borne everything, made all the decisions…and endured each painful consequence without anyone to take an ounce of the load from her delicate shoulders. Mike would never have wanted her to carry that burden alone. Nick didn't like her enduring so much hardship and loneliness, especially when he could handle it and had more experience with criminals.

"Thank you, doctor." Sasha fidgeted nervously. "Is there anything you can give Harper to help her or make her more comfortable for now?"

After a recommendation of acetaminophen and an over-the-counter nasal decongestant, along with rest and vitamins, the doctor tucked her equipment away. "I hope she feels better."

"We'll let you know if we need anything else," Nick assured.

When the doctor shouldered her way past him and out the door, Sasha eased Harper back into bed, looking as if she was fighting tears.

"She's worse than you thought." Nick read her distress.

"Yes."

"You look too overwrought to make decisions, so I'll tell you what I see as your best course of action. Leave Harper with the Santiagos to recover while you come with me to figure out what proof Mike stashed and where."

Sasha looked horrified. And ready to scream. She puffed up. Color raced to her cheeks as she squared her shoulders for battle.

Instead of screeching the *no* on the tip of her tongue, she grabbed him by the shirt and dragged him out of the bedroom, away from her daughter. In the hallway, she looked both ways in indecision, then tugged him toward the master—the only place in the house where no one would overhear them.

When she slammed the door and shoved him against it, Nick couldn't deny that he was impressed—and harder than he'd like to admit.

"Look, I agreed to whore myself, to let you use my body however you want, to protect my daughter. I will *not* leave her with strangers. If you keep trying to separate her from me, I'll—"

Sasha pressed her lips shut, as if realizing she was about to make a threat she couldn't carry out.

Nick didn't call her on it. Instead, he softened his voice. "I've known the Santiagos for years. They're solid, I swear."

"You swear? I don't trust you, so your opinion means nothing. I won't do it."

He didn't take pleasure in her distress, but he was glad to see her fighting spirit. She'd need it to make the right choice and survive the days ahead.

"Sasha, how will Harper recover if we drag her to hell and back? I'm sure Mike hid his evidence well. Searching every logical spot could take days…weeks. Some places we'll have to search in the dead of night when they're dark and deserted. Are you going to leave Harper back at whatever low-grade motel we crash in? Or wake her up, slow down her recovery, and risk our detection to bring her with us?" he challenged.

"I don't know right now." He heard the fear and frustration in her voice. "I'll figure it out. But I'm all Harper has. All she's ever known. I can't abandon her. She'll be terrified. She's just a baby."

"You know Clifford is dangerous or you wouldn't have come here and agreed to my terms." He raised a brow at her. "Harper will be safe with the Santiagos. That bastard and his thugs will never connect your daughter to my friends. But if we take her with us and we're caught, what do you think will happen?"

She looked away, refusing to answer.

"What do you think they'll do to Harper?" he pressed on.

Sasha closed her eyes and tensed. "Don't."

"I'm sorry to be blunt, but you might as well put a bullet in her head yourself. She's your daughter, so it's your call." He shook off her hold and opened the bedroom door. "Let me know what you decide. We're leaving tonight."

* * * *

The sun sank toward the horizon as Sasha's dread climbed. She had to make a decision.

She watched Harper on a blanket in the middle of the floor, clutching a new teddy bear under one arm as she scribbled with a fresh box of crayons across a pristine coloring book. At the moment, her daughter played more like a typical kid than she had in…well, ever.

Sasha swallowed and glanced at London on the sofa beside her. "Thank you for bringing Harper some toys. You didn't have to—"

"It was our pleasure." London grinned. "It gives my husbands a glimpse into our future."

Sasha wondered how and why a woman with a seemingly sweet disposition and an air of innocence had fallen for two brothers. Not that she was judging. Little shocked her anymore. She'd spent years in New Orleans, in the heart of the Quarter, where most anything was not only possible but happened regularly.

Dulce cried in fussy whines and pants. The Santiago brothers passed her back and forth, doing their best with voices and funny faces to make their daughter smile. They loved her madly, and it showed.

Sasha's chest tightened. Harper would never know a father's love. Mike was gone forever, and Sasha couldn't imagine a future in which she met another man she'd choose to share her life—or her daughter—with.

"She's hungry," she murmured to the pretty blonde with the big, winking diamond on her ring finger.

"Yep. Some things a mother just knows." London paused. "Listen, I realize the choice in front of you is gut-wrenching. In your shoes, I'd be falling apart. I love my husbands more than life…but the love a woman feels for her child is something else altogether. So pure and unbreakable."

Sasha nodded, too close to tears to speak. She'd been turning this dilemma over in her head all day. She felt nothing but tied up in knots.

London laid a hand over hers. "Your daughter will be safe with us. I'll be with her. Javier and Xander are protectors, and I guarantee their first call once we leave here will be to Xander's bestie, Logan. He's a former Navy SEAL with twin daughters of his own. Logan will fix us up with the best damn bodyguards in the state. No one will let anything happen to Harper."

Though that eased her mind some, Sasha bit her lip. "All that would turn your life upside down. And the expense—"

"Sasha, Nick once helped my husbands and me in desperate times. I wouldn't be alive today if that man hadn't stepped in. We can never repay him. This is the one and only favor he's ever asked of us. You and Harper are important to him, so you're important to us. Besides, your daughter is so precious. It will be a privilege to keep her safe while she recovers."

Sasha was running out of reasons to refuse except the thought of being separated from her baby wrenched her heart. But refusing the Santiagos' offer wouldn't be best for her daughter, just easier for her own peace of mind. "You're not worried about Dulce getting sick?"

"I can keep the girls apart until Harper is better. Frankly, that's one of the perks of having two husbands."

A smile flitted across London's glowing face as if she paused to remember some of the other undoubtedly pleasurable perks of being married to two handsome, rich men.

Sasha cast a glance over at Nick. He watched her intently. At times, he seemed ruthless, like the hardened criminal she'd expected. And sometimes, he didn't seem like a bad guy at all. He was definitely dangerous; Mike hadn't been wrong about that. But even with Nick's audacious sexual demands, he didn't seem dangerous to *her*. And if she was honest, the memory of him on top of her, pinning her down, gaze penetrating hers, made her breath catch.

God, she was in way over her head. The situation—Clifford, the danger, Harper's illness, Nick's demands, her own crazy attraction to him—was spinning beyond her control. She had to start making some decisions now. Dithering could get everyone killed.

"Let us help watch Harper for you," London implored, then cast a sidelong glance across the room. "You and Nick are up to your eyeballs in trouble, and I'm worried what will happen if you take your daughter along. We owe Nick. You're the only other thing I've ever seen him care about. You need him…and I think he needs you."

Sasha resisted that notion. "I don't have anything left to give him."

"You do." London didn't spell it out, just looked as if she knew the truth and thought Sasha was being a coward for not facing it.

"I'm helping him take Clifford down. That's all he needs."

"Don't you want revenge, too? That crooked bastard killed your husband."

Of course Sasha wanted vengeance for Mike, but she owed her daughter a normal childhood. So far, all Harper had known was being homeless, dirt poor, and afraid. Maybe…if she and Nick managed the seemingly impossible, her baby could someday have a home and toys and a safe school in a lovely neighborhood. Maybe Harper would forget all about this terrible time in their lives.

"All right. I'll go." Sasha's voice shook. "Harper can stay with you."

With a sigh of relief, London laid a gentle hand on her shoulder. "Thank God. I know that was a tough decision. I promise, we'll do everything in our power to protect her."

"I believe you." And Sasha did. Something about London's demeanor told her the woman had overcome devastation. Because London understood pain and suffering, she would never heap them on anyone else.

The blonde hugged her. Then Sasha heard London's soft voice in her ear. "Nick needs you in other ways. Don't be afraid of whatever is between you. He's a good guy with a crappy past who got framed for a vicious crime. What he needs most isn't your help, but your caring."

Before Sasha could reply, London backed away and cozied up next to Harper on the floor. Blinking, Sasha stared. What could she say? The only thing between her and Nick right now was Mike's missing evidence and her agreement to be his mistress for the month.

She lifted her gaze to the man. A tingling wave of awareness spread through her. Hunger darkened his face. Her heart careened wildly. Would he want the first installment of his payment tonight?

"Sasha?" he asked, glancing at London playing with Harper on the blanket.

"She's not coming with us." Sasha knew she would fall apart when the time came to leave her baby—her most important reason for living—behind.

"Good." He nodded her way, then glanced out the window. "It will be dark in thirty. We'll leave then."

That meant she had to pack up the clothes Nick had washed for Harper, along with the pretty new things the Santiagos had apparently brought and her new medicine. In less than five minutes, she was handing a little bag to London, then pulling Harper into her lap.

God, the thought of leaving her baby hurt. She asked herself again what kind of mother would leave her daughter, but the answer was simple: the sort who wanted her child to live.

"Baby, you're going to go spend a few days with Ms. London and Dulce. They have lots of toys and I'll bet if you asked, they'd feed you some ice cream. Okay?"

"Icth cream?" Harper's face lit up, her smile so much like Mike's.

She nodded. "Does that sound good?"

Harper bobbed her head excitedly.

"We'll have lots of fun," London promised.

"Yeah!" Harper hugged the teddy bear in her grip.

It seemed like a blink later that Xander cradled a sleeping Dulce and hustled his brother out the door. Their wife followed, carrying all of Harper's worldly belongings on her shoulder and holding the little girl's hand. To Sasha's surprise, Harper didn't cling to her mother, just hugged her.

"I'll miss you," Sasha whispered.

"Miss you, mama." The girl planted a sweet kiss on her cheek. "Come back soon?"

Sasha certainly hoped so, but she refused to make a promise she might not be able to keep. "I'll do my very best."

"Who wants chicken nuggets for dinner?" London distracted the girl.

With one last squeeze, Harper turned back to the other woman. "With frewnch fries?"

London laughed. "Of course."

"I love you," Sasha called out to her baby.

"Love you." Harper waved, more intent on London's promise of fried food.

As her daughter disappeared around the corner, London looked her way with a silent promise that Harper would be safe.

Thank you, she mouthed.

Then they were gone.

Sasha pressed her lips together and gripped the threshold, doing her best not to fall to her knees and sob. What if she never saw her daughter again?

Suddenly, Nick wrapped strong hands around her shoulders and braced her. He drew her back against his big chest and cradled her. "Harper will be all right."

He said that like it was a fact.

"I haven't been away from her since she was fifteen months old." When Sasha closed her eyes, tears leaked from the corners.

Mike's funeral. She'd left her daughter with a neighbor during the graveside service because it had been scorching and cloying and pouring down rain. With every word from the minister's lips, she'd been silently praying to God to help Mike's soul rest easy and to keep Harper safe.

"It's better for her," Nick reminded her in a calm voice.

Sasha knew that. It just didn't feel that way. "We're leaving here?"

"Now," he confirmed as he released her.

She suddenly felt cold again. "I'm ready. I already gathered my things."

It took less than two minutes for him to shut off all the lights, grab their bags, and lead her out into the alley.

The evening was crisp. Sasha pulled her sweater tighter around her. Nick watched everything around them as he slung his backpack and her duffel over his shoulder and guided her down the road with a hot palm at her back.

In fifteen silent minutes, they reached a parking garage. Nick sneaked his way around the security guard, ducked under a series of video surveillance cameras, then crept through the shadows and up the stairs until they reached a black SUV on the third floor, near an executive entrance door.

Glancing one last time over his shoulder, Nick knelt to grab the keys from a magnetic box under the wheel well and unlocked the vehicle with a beep. He opened the passenger door. "Get in."

She did as he stowed their bags. "How are we going to get out without being seen?"

"Easy," he assured as he climbed in beside her. "The license plate is registered to the corporation. Vehicle's new."

She could smell the pristine leather and off-the-factory-floor parts. "So?"

"The windows are tinted. No one will be able to see us. I'm sure it's equipped with a sticker to get us out of this garage without having to even roll down a window. The question is, where are we going? What do you know?"

While Nick backed out of the parking spot and the SUV glided down the ramp, she tried to recollect everything she'd done to solve the puzzle Mike had left her. Nick's big fingers around the steering wheel distracted her. His thumb tapped the leather beneath—the same thumb he'd brushed across her nipple last night. She shivered with pleasure at the memory.

True to his word, when they reached the exit, the security arm lifted without them having to engage the guard at the exit.

"Sasha?"

His deep voice demanded an answer. She didn't know what to say. "I've been over and over this. He left me a message, and I'm still not sure what it means."

"Tell me."

Wringing her hands, Sasha tried to squelch hope from burgeoning again. So many times over the past interminable months, she'd thought she had the answer to this mystery. Failure dashed her every time. She wasn't sure if she could take it again.

On the other hand, she had no choice. Her future—and her daughter's—depended on it.

"The day before Mike's murder, he arranged to have flowers sent to the house on what became the day of his funeral. Inside the envelope was a card that didn't make any sense and this." She pulled up a long chain she'd tucked under her shirt with a mysterious key attached.

Nick reached over and slid the key into his palm. She felt the heat of his hand radiating to her chest. A jolt of something more than awareness fluttered through Sasha. It refused to subside, no matter how much she tensed against it.

A bump in the road jerked them. His knuckles brushed the swells of her breasts. A gasp slipped out before she could stop it.

His stare zipped up to her, and she felt caught. Could he see her heart pounding? Feel her nipples beading?

Suddenly, he released the key and leaned back into his seat, focused on the dark road ahead. "What did the card say?"

Sasha tried to string two thoughts together. "Um, gibberish, really. Something about it being Han Solo's turn to stop Darth Vader by finding the ammunition in the Death Star. He even signed the card as Luke Skywalker."

Frowning, Nick heaved a long sigh. "That sly motherfucker."

She tensed, searching his pensive face. "What do you mean? Did that make sense to you."

Nick nodded. "I know where he hid his evidence. Sit back. We're heading to New Orleans."

Chapter Three

Near the airport off I-10, Nick checked them into an old motel unlikely to have much in the way of high-tech security. Midnight had just fallen. Despite napping in the car, Sasha looked damn near ready to collapse. Her eyelids drooped. Her shoulders sagged. How long had it been since she'd had a decent night's sleep? Since she'd felt safe enough to have one?

After he parked around back, in a spot not visible from the road, he pushed his way into the dingy room and glanced back cautiously. No one inhabited the parking lot. No one had followed.

Shouldering his way past Sasha, he drew his gun and prowled around the room, checking every corner and closet. Empty. "Come in. Shut the door. Lock and deadbolt it."

She did, her gaze skittering over the kitchenette, the loveseat in front of the vintage TV, grimy windows, and crappy carpet. Nick saw the instant she realized the room had one bed. He'd done it to keep her close. And because he'd been a stupid bastard too tempted to pass up the opportunity to hold her, even if all they did was sleep. It had been a long time since he'd just breathed in a female and held her body against his. And he craved touching this woman.

"Now what?" Sasha made her way into the room, her nervous gaze jerky, her respiration unsteady. "Are we going to the location tonight?"

Nick shook his head. "I need to call Xander for a little help first. I also need to ask you some questions."

"Me? I've told you everything."

"That you think is relevant," he corrected. "Tell me about the week leading up to Mike's death. His body was discovered on Friday morning, right?"

Nick already knew the answer to that. The moment he'd heard the news—one of his last while out on bail—was forever seared in his brain. His rigged trial had begun the day of Mike's murder. The evening he'd learned of his friend's demise, he'd officially become a convicted rapist.

Wasn't the timing ironic?

"Yes. But I knew something was wrong on Wednesday night," she said. "He came home late. He was too quiet. Very distracted. When I asked if he was all right, he said something had happened at work and he didn't want to talk about it. After dinner, he sequestered himself in his home office. He didn't come to bed until…late."

"He called me that Wednesday night and told me that Clifford was onto him. He wanted to know how to protect you and Harper." Nick shook his head. "I instructed him to leave you a list of account names, passwords, and contacts, so you'd have ready cash and help."

That had her gaping in surprise. "You did?"

He nodded. "Mike was afraid for his safety but he was more worried about you two."

"That sounds like him. He didn't come home Thursday night. Didn't answer texts or phone calls. I left voice mails…" Sasha fought tears valiantly. "In the middle of the night, I started looking through his home office for clues. At first, I wondered if he had a lover or something, but the night before…" She blushed, and Nick could guess that Mike had made love to his wife, fearing it would be the last time. "In the top drawer, in an envelope with my name written on the front, sat a letter which accounted for every dime we had saved. I knew something terrible had happened then. A police office knocked on my door a few hours later."

Goddamn it. "I'm sorry. I promised Mike I'd take care of you. Even as my trial was going on, I hoped I wouldn't actually be convicted." And he felt like shit that he'd been dumb enough to be framed and had been unable to keep his promise. "I hoped truth and logic would prevail. I never even got to testify on my own behalf and bring up the fact that Fiona was Clifford's niece or that I'd been investigating the crooked DA. I found out later that the bastard had threatened my attorney's children."

Sasha looked stunned. "How is Clifford still holding office?"

Nick grimaced. "Like all successful politicians, he smiles well, placates his special interests, and is a damn good liar."

"Well…all that detailed information you told him to leave me was a saving grace. After Mike's funeral that Monday, I withdrew every dime we had. I put the house up for sale, quit my job, sold my car, withdrew Harper from preschool. Clifford's goons threatened me before we could go underground with our stash of cash. I've had some close calls since then. There was once I would have sworn we wouldn't escape—" She bit back the rest, as if she'd rather forget.

"It's all right." He caressed her shoulder, then paced to the chair across the room. "I just wish like hell I'd gotten out sooner or been able to talk to you. It would have saved you a lot of shit."

"You really know where Mike stashed his evidence?" She breathed as if his assertion was too good to believe.

He nodded. "I'm pretty sure. Did Mike ever tell you how we met?"

"He said you beat up some bullies who were bothering him."

A little smile tugged at his lips. "Mike and I probably should never have been friends. He was a scrawny thirteen-year-old from swanky Lakeshore Drive. I was a seventeen-year-old with a record who lived near the projects. My dad had run off, and my mom moved us here from Jersey. She thought it would be romantic to live in New Orleans." He snorted. "It would have been better if she'd had a job and some cash saved. They should never have called that shithole we moved to Desire; no one wanted to live there. But Mike and some church youth group came to the 'hood on a do-gooder mission to change our lives for an afternoon or whatever. He got separated from his adult handler. He was so shiny that he looked rich, and some of the kids on my block were shaking him down for the goodies in his pockets and beating the hell out of him in the process."

"You stopped them," Sasha murmured, cocking her head as if she was seeing him for the first time.

Nick didn't want her getting the idea that he was any sort of hero. "I don't like an unfair fight. I evened the odds, is all."

"But you didn't have to. You chose to." She sent him a dissecting frown. "Just like you could have shut the door in my face last night. Or taken advantage of me when I was on my knees. Why didn't you?"

"I'm an opportunistic prick, not a heartless bastard. I'm not going to keep a sick kid in the rain." He scowled. "Do you want to hear the rest of this or not?"

She crossed her arms over her chest and paced away from him, bristling at his tone. He mentally filed away that trick to keep distance between them. "Carry on."

"After I got the kids in the 'hood to back off, I helped Mike return to his group. After that, he and his family kind of…adopted me. Jeanine tried to mother me."

That made Sasha smile. "My mother-in-law tried to mother everyone. Mike was crushed when she passed away."

Nick had been when he'd heard, too. "At least the heart attack was fast. Mike's dad was a great guy. He often tried to give me guidance back then since my old man took off."

"Glen is lonely in that home, I'm sure. I've wished a million times that I could visit him, but I don't dare risk putting him in danger. He probably thinks I've deserted him."

Same here. Nick had never had the balls to tell the old man that he'd managed to add to his rap sheet. Even if the conviction had been pure bullshit, he hadn't wanted to see the censure on the old man's face. "When this is over, I'll go see him. I'm sure he misses Mike like hell."

She nodded. "I'll take Harper to see him. He'd like that. Sorry to keep getting us sidetracked. So they kind of took you in…"

"Yeah, when Glen was still running the freight company, he was having some theft problems. I helped him figure out who was robbing him blind. He suggested I become a P.I." Nick shrugged. "It stuck. So I owe him. But you know Mike had a major *Star Wars* thing as a kid, right?"

She huffed. "As an adult, too. God, he loved that stuff. It killed me to sell all his LEGO collectible sets and figurines."

"But you couldn't take it with you, and you needed the money."

"Yeah. I was shocked to find out that the LEGO Death Star thing from 2005 was worth over twenty-five hundred dollars."

"If he'd bought the damn Millennium Falcon LEGO set, like I told him to, back in 2007, that sucker is worth sixteen grand now." Nick shook his head because even he couldn't believe the value of little plastic pieces. "Anyway, when he was a kid, we would meet in City Park a lot. He'd ride his bike down from Lakeshore, usually accompanied by Jeanine. We often hung out at Popp Bandstand. Know where that is?"

"Yes. I had my bridal pictures taken there."

He would bet she'd looked beautiful in white lace and innocence with one of the city's most delicate structures as her backdrop. "During summer evenings, we'd stay late. Sometimes a live band would play."

"The city is so full of music. That's one thing I loved about it when I moved here."

"Yeah. And fireworks would light up the sky. That's when Mike loved to pretend he was Luke Skywalker. I was Han Solo. We were in a raging battle, and the bandstand was the Death Star. He was going to be the hero, by god. I helped."

"You indulged a kid. Most teenagers would have ignored him."

Being with Mike had given him the opportunity to be a kid again, too. He'd barely gotten the chance to be one since his dad had taken off and money had become scarce. "I liked him."

"He was a wonderful man and I miss him every day."

Of course. She'd loved him. Mike had always been a lucky bastard.

"Me, too," Nick murmured.

"So you think the evidence is somewhere around the bandstand?"

"Yeah. But I need to call Xander, see if he can find out about the surveillance in the area, if there are any upcoming events... That kind of thing. It's a public place, and there's a coffee house nearby. It's likely someone will see us. We have to seem as inconspicuous as possible, try not to draw too much attention."

"We can ask him about Harper, too, right?"

She must worry about her daughter like crazy. How wonderful would it be for someone to miss him half that much? "Sure."

As he drew out his phone, she disappeared into the room's little bath. He heard the splash of water, a long sigh. Sasha was trying to keep herself together. Nick would rather she leaned on him, but he knew why she wouldn't. And it was better this way. Less emotional, fewer opportunities to trip on temptation. Comforting her could be disastrous for his self-control.

Thankfully, Xander answered on the first ring, distracting him. "You there?"

"Yeah. I need another favor."

"I need a new head of security," the younger Santiago quipped. "Can we work something out?"

"Bastard. Focus." Nick asked his questions about Popp Bandstand. "Can you find that out?"

On the other end of the line, he could hear Xander clicking. "I don't see any events in the next forty-eight hours. I can't tell you about surveillance, man. Finding that information would take me getting behind a firewall or something, and you know I'm a lover, not a hacker."

Damn it. And Nick didn't have a computer with him so he could tap into the city's security. "Every female north of Lake Pontchartrain knows that, man. And a few south, too, I'm sure."

"I only have eyes for my wife now."

With anyone else, Nick would have called bullshit, but from everything he'd seen, Xander was dead serious. "Mike left Sasha a key. I have no idea what it belongs to. Anything in the area that makes sense? It would have to be something he felt sure no one would disturb for months…years."

"I haven't been to New Orleans in a while. Sorry. I'll ask Javier. If he can think of something, I'll ring you back."

Sasha emerged from the bathroom. Their eyes met. Hers pleaded. Nick wished she wanted him half as much as she wanted his phone right now but he couldn't afford to be a dumb, desperate fidiot. Jesus, why hadn't he managed to get laid before she'd knocked on his door last night? On the other hand, would it have mattered?

"Great," he said to Xander. "I'm going to pass you to Sasha so she can ask you about Harper."

"Sure. Good kid. She seems to be doing better."

Nick was glad to hear it. She probably had Mike's disposition, too. "Talk to you later."

When he handed the phone to Sasha, she clutched it like a lifeline. "Hi. How's Harper?"

Xander must have said something reassuring because she smiled as if someone had lifted a megaton weight from her slender shoulders.

Cupping her elbow, Nick snagged her attention. "I'm running to the drugstore down the street. I think I've got a plan to get us into the park without raising too many eyebrows. Hungry?"

She shook her head. "The burger filled me up."

He nodded. "Lock up behind me. Don't answer the door for anyone else. I'll be back."

She gave him an absent nod, then turned her attention to the call once more. "So she fell right asleep? Is the medicine helping? Did she cry at bedtime?"

He slipped out the door, hearing the click of the deadbolt, and hit the twenty-four hour pharmacy nearby, grabbing supplies with a bit of help and tossing them into the basket. When he got to the cashier, Nick figured Sasha wouldn't like everything he'd bought…but better safe than sorry. And if she wanted to fight about it, he would handle that, too.

* * * *

When Sasha let him in the motel room, she was still clutching the phone with a warm smile.

"Everything all right?" Nick asked, gripping the bag from the drugstore.

"Yeah. Xander filled me in. Harper's fever is coming down. She's been sitting in bed most of the evening, watching movies she's never had the opportunity to see. Apparently she loves *Frozen*."

Nick wasn't entirely sure what that was, but hearing the news that her daughter behaved like a typical little girl seemed to fill Sasha with relief.

"And they're reading her some books, too. She loves them." Sasha bit her lip. "She's missed out on so many normal childhood things."

"Don't blame yourself. Clifford is the one who fucked up your life."

She winced, and Nick realized belatedly that she probably hadn't heard that kind of language too much. Mike had never been one to swear. He remembered him once saying that Sasha had grown up very sheltered with small-town, religious parents. Nick resisted the urge to shake his head in self-reproach. His first spoken word had probably contained four letters.

"Sorry," he mumbled.

"No. You're right. I didn't want this life for Harper. For myself. I certainly wanted more than an early grave for Mike." She sighed. "But Walter Clifford changed all that, and it's too late to undo his damage. All we can do is try to pick up and move on. Will something in the bag help us accomplish that?"

She reached for the items he'd procured at the drugstore. Nick thought about stopping her, shielding her. He didn't. Better that she understand now. "To start, yes."

When he handed the sack to her, she peeked in. Pausing, she frowned as she grabbed the first of two matching boxes. "Hair color? Rich dark brown?"

"Clifford is looking for a blonde with a toddler, not a brunette with a boyfriend."

Sasha zipped her stare to him, her lush lips parted in surprise. "A what?"

"Boyfriend. Me. We're going to the bandstand about midmorning, after the joggers but before the stroll-through-the-park-at-lunch crowd. The moms pushing strollers that time of day won't pay us much mind. If Clifford has surveillance on the area, all he'll see is two people hand in hand, seemingly in love." He picked up the Saints ball cap he'd bought and shoved it on his head. "Not only will you look different, but by tomorrow morning, I'll have enough stubble to pass as a beard. With the bill over my face and these"—he extracted a pair of cheap, dark sunglasses, tag dangling—"no one will recognize me. You have a pair in there, too."

"And makeup?" She ignored the glasses and started pulling cosmetics from the bag.

He shrugged, hoping he hadn't fucked up. "One of the female clerks helped me."

Sasha studied the BB cream that was supposed to adjust to her skin tone, the soft peachy-pink blush, and a translucent powder. A little compact with some brown, gold, and rosy shadows pressed into the shape of an eye shimmered behind the plastic lid.

"The woman said these colors would work for most anyone. When I told her you had hazel eyes, she recommended those shadows."

"You remembered?"

The color of her eyes? Yeah, he'd never forgotten. "There's a nude lip in there, too. Whatever that means."

Nick wished like hell Sasha would give him some sort of reaction. Was she pleased? Pissed? Or just puzzled?

Suddenly, she smiled at him. "This is the most makeup I've had in what seems like forever. Oh, the lipstick looks pretty. Mascara!" She hugged it to her chest. "I've missed this. Thanks."

He sighed with relief as she pulled out a couple of toothbrushes, toothpaste, a new brush, a travel-sized lotion. "You're welcome. Sasha—"

"What's this?" she asked of the last item in the bag.

He saw the instant she realized what he'd bought. She turned a rosy shade and set the box on the counter carefully.

"Condoms," he confirmed, still not sure whether he'd bought them to remind her of his "demand" so this mood between them would be less cozy...or just in case his restraint didn't last.

For a long minute, she didn't say anything. Finally, she swallowed as if she worked up her courage and looked at him. "Thank you for thinking of protecting me. Am I coloring my hair now or in the morning?"

Despite her matter-of-fact reply, Nick had to work not to get hard while thinking about Sasha and condoms in the same sentence. No luck.

He turned away. "In the morning is fine. I'm going to take a shower. Make sure the motel door is locked."

Without waiting for her reply, Nick disappeared into the bathroom. He stripped down, soaped up, and stroked himself to climax, biting back a groan at the thought of crushing Sasha's delicate mouth under his as he surged deep inside her. Self-pleasure barely shaved down the edge of his need, but better to work off as much as he could before he crawled in bed beside her.

Cursing, he wrapped a towel around his waist and jerked the door open. His backpack with his clean underwear was still on the bed, and he'd forgotten—

The sight in front of him zapped every fucking thought from his head.

"Sasha?"

She'd folded down the ratty bedspread and eased between the starched white sheets, sitting with her knees tucked under her, ass resting on her soles. She wore a sleeveless white nightgown that ended just above her knees. Sheer lace trimmed the gentle slope of fabric covering her breasts and the hem at the bottom. It was plain as hell and not meant to be sexy in the least. But it was probably all she had. She had unfastened the top two buttons of the garment, revealing a hint of her shadowy cleavage.

Jacking off in the shower had been futile.

Bowed head, hands clasped, Nick watched her shoulders rise and fall with every nervous breath. She looked like a goddamn sacrificial virgin.

"I'm ready," Sasha whispered.

No, she wasn't.

Nick rubbed at the back of his neck. "Listen—"

"Mike told me once that you like to be...in charge. In bed."

Damn his old pal. "Sasha—"

"I can be..." She grappled for words. "Compliant."

He snorted. Unless she could be eager, he would never touch her. "Look at me."

Sasha blinked up, clearly confused—until she caught sight of him.

She gasped. Her eyes bulged, her stare walking all over him. Her mouth hung open.

Her visual worship gave his ego a boost. Knowing she liked what she saw got his dick harder, too. But it didn't really change anything between them.

"What the hell are you doing?" he asked.

"Well...you've done everything you said you would to keep Harper and me safe. We made a deal." She was breathing hard. "You gave me last night to be with her. Now I'm living up to my end of the bargain."

He noticed she hadn't said she was dying to have his cock inside her tight pussy as she clawed her way to climax.

"Have you ever had sex with a man other than Mike?"

"No."

"You ever had a man eat your pussy until you're so sensitive you had to plead to make him stop?"

Her cheeks went rosier. "No."

"You ever wanted a man so much you begged him to fuck you until your throat felt raw?"

"No." Her voice turned breathier.

"You ever come so hard you weren't sure you had any bones left in your thoroughly melted body?"

Sasha's saucer-wide eyes told him she wondered if such reactions were even possible. "No."

"Ever even fantasized about those things?"

Her gaze dropped to her lap again. She swallowed. "Why all the questions?"

"Yes or no?"

"I agreed to give you my body, not my mind."

Nick had no right, but that answer pissed him off. If he was going to risk her hatred and his own self-loathing, then by god he wanted all of her.

He grabbed her chin in his grip and forced her gaze up to his. "If you can't even answer me, then you're not ready for the way I intend to fuck you. Not even close."

Sasha jerked from his grip. "What more do you want? You can force me to spread my legs for you and give you everything between them. You can't force me to share everything under my skin."

With a jolt, Nick realized that's exactly what he wanted—her thoughts, her consideration, her heart—and he was never going to get them.

"Until you can give me all that, don't offer me your body again," he said softly.

"I'll never share those deep parts of myself with another man. I loved Mike."

Nick had known that, but hearing her say the words still stabbed him deep. "Then we have nothing else to say. Go to bed."

Another outburst sat on the tip of her tongue. It was all over her face, but she stifled it, jerking down to lay on her side, back to him, and yanked the covers to her neck.

"Fine." She reached up and turned off the dingy lamp on her nightstand, killing the bit of glow in the room. "But how are we possibly going to convince anyone tomorrow that we're in love?"

Because she couldn't pretend that she didn't loathe him. Message received loud and clear. He'd gotten what he wanted—for her to think he was a douchebag and to keep her distance—so he shouldn't pout like a bitch about it now.

That didn't mean he liked the corner he'd wedged himself into one bit.

Nick turned off his own lamp. "Sasha?"

"What?"

The parking lot lamp outside their window lit the room just well enough to see her outline in the bed beside him. He grabbed her wrist and tugged her onto her back. An instant later, he was on her, sinking his fingers into her hair, breathing her name against her lips as he captured her mouth with his own.

Chapter Four

Sasha was already suffering from a soft ache between her legs when Nick began asking pointed questions in sexual growls. When his long fingers scorched their way around her wrist, her blood had caught fire. Then suddenly, she'd found herself lying flat on her back, staring breathlessly into his midnight eyes as he silently dismantled her defenses.

You ever wanted a man so much you begged him to fuck you until your throat felt raw?

Was he saying he could do that to her?

She was still wondering the answer to that question when he dragged her beneath him. With a fist in her hair, he tilted her head until his mouth loomed right above her own. She knew what he intended. Nick Navarro was going to kiss her.

She gasped, part surprise, part protest. He didn't worry, pause, or care why she squeaked out the sound. He ignored everything but her mouth as his lips seized hers unerringly in the dark. No fumbling. No hesitation. No lack of confidence. And absolutely no lack of skill. Just the thorough caress of his shockingly soft lips, proving without any doubt that he was determined to take and taste her, to lay claim to her until she surrendered every bit of herself to him and his will.

Oh, my goodness gracious...

He didn't bother to hold in his groan as he shifted closer and nudged her lips apart. It wasn't a polite request that she let him in but a demand, pure and simple. His kiss lit a passion she'd not only thought dead, but roared into a sizzling torch she'd never even known existed.

He delved in with his tongue, taking command. Owning her. Slowly, shyly, she curled her fingers around his steely shoulders and parted her mouth to invite him deeper.

You ever come so hard you weren't sure you had any bones left in your thoroughly melted body?

No. Not once. But when he asked the question that way, she'd sure like to feel it.

His fingers tightened in her hair. His lips crushed hers. He possessed her. She couldn't move a muscle beneath Nick without him sensing her every nuance and positioning her so he could open her wider, take more, coax her completely.

Her heartbeat filled her head. Even lying flat, a dizzy thrill she'd never experienced utterly overwhelmed her. She couldn't speak a word, catch a single breath, process a whole thought. God, it was wonderful.

His musky scent filled her nose, expanded into her head, crowded out reason. And she didn't care. Pleasure had her floating yet anchored to him. His kiss melted her like chocolate, addicted her like drugs.

Sasha lifted to him, closer, now whimpering not in surprise but entreaty as her blood sizzled under her skin and scorched through her veins.

When he eased back, she panicked, clawed at his shoulders. That couldn't be it. She wasn't ready to give up these sensations, couldn't let him go. Desperate, she felt her way up the strong column of his neck, squeezing, panting, aching.

"Nick…" She didn't even know what she was asking for. Harder. Sweeter. Faster. Deeper. Softer. Wilder. More of him and everything his dirty, rough, pointed questions had insinuated he could give her.

He didn't answer, just slanted her another dominant stare that vowed untold pleasure and ruined her for abstinence. His breath heaved in and out of his wide chest as he yanked loose the next three buttons of her eyelet lace nightie.

"Baby, one taste…I knew it would never be enough. Give me more. I want those pretty nipples."

She'd barely comprehended Nick's words when his fingers slid under the fabric—right toward her peaked tip. Everything in her body tensed in expectation. He was going to touch the bare flesh only Mike ever had. He was going to make her mindless with need.

He cupped a blistering palm around her breast, his thumb razing a fiery path across her nipple. She dragged in a stuttered, shocked breath, her stare fixed on him. His touch felt suffused with a magic she didn't understand. If it was an illusion, she didn't want to know the trick, just experience his sleight-of-hand over and over.

"Fuck," he muttered against her lips, then dipped in for another taste as if he couldn't stay away. "Every time I look at you, I want to touch you. Now that I have my hands on you, I don't know how I'll stop."

Right now, she didn't care if he ever did.

Sasha arched into his hand. He squeezed her nipple between his thumb and forefinger. A jolt of sensation zipped between her legs. She pressed her thighs together, aching for something she suspected only Nick could give her.

He undid another button at the front of her gown and dragged it off one shoulder, exposing her left breast. He folded the oversized garment down to expose the other. Her peaks beaded up even more, and she couldn't strictly blame the chill.

Could he see? Did he know how much her body yearned for him right now?

With a guttural moan, he cradled her right breast in his hand and dipped his head. He wasn't going to merely kiss her; he intended to put her nipple in his mouth.

Her heart pounded against her ribs as his lips closed around her engorged nub. Another shock of pleasure zapped her. She rose to him, wrapping her seeking hands around his head and dragging him closer. She didn't dare speak. Heck, she barely dared to breathe.

Then his tongue… *Oh, my.* Yes, he flicked her nipple with that wickedly soft blade. Tingles scattered, swirled, gathered, and pooled right between her legs, adding to the gnawing ache throbbing there in a way Sasha had never really experienced.

She and Mike had loved each other, and their sex had reflected their sweet, comforting relationship. The way Nick Navarro touched her was raw, dirty, urgent…compelling.

Restlessly, his tongue wandered over her flesh again, licking his way up the valley between her breasts, nipping at her neck before he stole his way into her mouth, then drifted back down to lave her left nipple and drown her in more mind-numbing bliss.

Sasha couldn't be still. Her legs moved restlessly beneath the covers, her hips lifting involuntarily, silently pleading for something she was afraid to name. Her fingertips glided over his massive shoulders, the power evident under his suede-soft skin potent. She followed her touch with soft kisses, spreading them across his hard shoulder and bulging biceps. He lifted his head and devoured her mouth again like he might starve to death if she didn't feed him her passion.

Then his hand skated between her cleavage, scored down her abdomen…then disappeared under the elastic of her panties.

The instant his fingers pried her folds apart and made contact with the most sensitive button on her body, she cried out, gripped him tight, and nearly fell apart.

"Jesus, you're wet." He panted every word, sending his harsh breath skittering over her skin.

She was. She could feel her moisture coating his exploring fingers. He glided his way down soft, sensitive skin before sinking a pair of fingers deep inside her and settling his thumb over her nubbin with soft, unrelenting strokes.

Sasha dug her nails into his arm. "Oh!"

"That's your clit, baby. I want to get so up-close and personal with it. Touch it." He circled the bundle of nerve endings with teasing slips of his fingers that had her spreading her legs, writhing for more, and feeling the blood flush her body with more desire. "Taste it. Make you plead. Make you scream. Make you come."

"Please." The word slipped from her lips.

Not once during the three years of her marriage to Mike had she ever begged him to give her pleasure. Barely twenty-four hours with Nick and she suddenly felt sure she would say or do most anything to purge the need brewing inside her, roiling just under his deft touch. She couldn't even pause to be shocked by her own response, by the fact that he seemed so capable of giving her the orgasm that had frequently eluded her in the past.

"I want to make you feel so good, baby. I took one look at you and I burned. I fucking fantasized about touching all that pristine skin, kissing you until you couldn't think, and feeling you come all over me."

"Nick…"

"Don't say my name now. Scream it when I send you over. That feel good? Yeah. You're close. I can tell."

He dragged his fingertips slowly over the pearl she could feel growing harder with every moment. Sensations built, gathering, heavy, pressing onto her resistance until it began crumbling. The ache in her body converged, morphing tingles and feel-good sensations into a craving that had her grabbing the sheets in her fists, panting wildly, and burning in need as she tossed her head back.

"Nick!" she shouted as her entire body pulsed and jerked. Liquid ecstasy jetted through her veins in surges that never seemed to end. She climbed even higher with his next stroke. Higher again with the one following. He always had his fingers exactly where she needed them, always petting her with the perfect pressure. God, the man already knew her body far better than she did. She hadn't even finished this mammoth orgasm and already she feared she'd sell her soul for more.

When the climax finally tapered off, her throat actually hurt from crying out his name. Languid euphoria rolled heavy satisfaction through her veins. Perspiration dampened her hairline. Her body hummed. Heck, she wouldn't be surprised if she was glowing.

Sasha smiled at him. "Nick…"

"Like that, huh?"

Somehow, she still blushed. "Couldn't you tell?"

"Yeah." He sat up, elbows braced on his knees, gripping his head in his hands, then sent her a pointed glance. "That was exactly what I wanted. Glad making you respond was easy. That's how we convince people we're in love."

He'd given her ecstasy to…what? Prove she wasn't immune to him? That he had power over her? Or to boost his ego? Manipulate her? He stared through her and shrugged, like nothing they'd done tonight had been out of the ordinary or meant a thing to him.

Sasha felt as if he'd slapped her.

"You bastard." She rolled away, putting her back to him. Shame stung as she buttoned her nightgown. Her fingers shook in anger.

"Bastard? I know it didn't take you this long to figure that out."

No. She had always suspected he was dangerous to a woman's sanity. Mike had warned her; Sasha wished she'd listened. Instead, she'd let her desperation to keep Harper alive mix dangerously with her attraction to Nick. Hope, loneliness, and need had run away with her.

Never again.

Feeling both violated and angry with herself for wanting him so badly, she curled into a self-protective ball. "Not at all."

"Good. You knew I was a bastard when you knocked on my door. I'm just living up to your expectation. After an orgasm like that, you ought to sleep good. 'Night."

* * * *

After six restless hours of dick-hardened hell, Nick rose with a groan. Sure, touching Sasha last night had been a fantasy come true, but everything afterward had been an utter clusterfuck. He had to stop wanting her so badly. If he couldn't, he'd have to continue behaving like an ass. Earning her contempt sucked. Worse, her nearness just kept wearing his resistance down. He was caught in an endless loop of shit, and his only way out was to find Mike's evidence or fuck her blind.

After Sasha's angry snit last night, he could guess which choice she would vote for.

It was a little after eight when he showered and self-pleasured again. Lamenting the frequent workout his hand was getting, he shoved on his underwear and tiptoed out of the bathroom to see if this rattrap had anything that made coffee.

Sasha stood beside the bed, looking both embarrassed and pissed as hell. He hated the former, but the latter would keep her the fuck away. Right now, he needed that because the way he'd pounced on her last night proved he couldn't rely on his own self-control.

"Need help with the hair dye?"

She hesitated, glaring at him for such a long time, he wondered if she was even speaking to him. "What do you know about coloring someone's hair?"

"Nothing. But I can read a box."

She pressed that rosy bow of a mouth into a straight line. "Fine. I'll talk you through the rest. Just don't touch me anywhere else."

Oh, feisty. She looked beautiful with flushed cheeks and sparks in her hazel eyes. Nick kept that to himself.

"Let's get to it. I want to blow this place quickly so we can grab some breakfast and be at the park by ten."

Sasha pried open the box, then removed two bottles and a tube. The last item she took to the shower. Then she unfolded the instructions, peeled off a pair of flimsy, clear gloves, and shoved them into his chest. "Put these on."

He barely had time to stare at the small plastic trappings and wonder how he was going to get his hands inside them when she brushed past him and started digging through her bag. A moment later, she came back with some claw-like clips. With the new brush, she sectioned off her hair into four quadrants, secured three of them in knots on her head, then mixed the two bottles together.

"I'm going to start with my hairline and the parts I just made. Watch. I'll squeeze the bottle gently. After that, you have to do the same all over to cover my roots and scalp. Once we've used all this up, I'll mix the other box so we can coat my hair all the way to my ends."

Nick really didn't understand much of what she said, but he shrugged as he wedged his hands into the gloves. He'd figure it out as he went along. "Sure."

Wordlessly, she pulled the other pair from the matching box and began applying the dark mixture at her widow's peak, working her way around her head and smoothing the dye back into her hair. When she reached her nape, she handed him the bottle with a sigh. "You'll have to get the back."

Wouldn't all the inmates back at the big house get a good laugh out of him playing hairdresser? Not that he gave a shit. He hadn't been there to make lifelong friends. He could do without a sliver of his man card for the morning if it avenged Mike and helped Sasha stay alive.

He did exactly as she asked, grabbing a hand towel when some of the goop ran down her neck. "Got it."

"Now you have to cover the majority of the roots and scalp." She demonstrated with the unbound section of her hair, taking small rows, applying a line of dye, working it in, then moving onto the next.

"That's it?"

She nodded. "It's easy. I used to do this for my mother. Even a kid can manage it."

In other words, so could an insensitive idiot. Nick would love to apologize. But if she softened toward him, that could be dangerous. Him in her pants was the last thing Mike would have wanted, and Nick knew he was bad for Sasha. She deserved a man who could provide the best of everything, would love her gently, and didn't have a record he could never shake.

Nick took the bottle and repeated everything she'd done through the remaining sections of her hair. By the time he was squeezing air from the bottle, she was already mixing up the next and shoving it into his hands.

"Work this through to the ends." She plucked up the shower cap from the little display of toiletries next to the sink. "Then I'll wrap it up for twenty minutes."

He nodded, working the rest of the gooey mixture into her strands until they were glossy and drenched. Normally, he'd take any opportunity to put his hands in her hair but this crap smelled somewhere between nasty and toxic. He was glad this would wash out in twenty-eight shampoos.

"Good enough," she declared as she snapped on the plastic shower cap. "Set a timer, please. Knock on the bathroom door when twenty minutes have passed."

The second he agreed, she grabbed her duffel and shoved him out. Moments later, he heard the shower running.

At the twenty-minute mark, he pounded on the door but the water still ran for another ten.

Another thirty minutes after that, Nick was glancing at his watch, wondering what the hell she was doing in there. Suddenly, she opened the door.

His jaw dropped.

She looked delicate and ethereal as a blonde. As a brunette, her eyes sparkled green, her skin glowed, and he'd have sworn she was one of the sexiest women he'd met in his fucking life. She'd applied the makeup with a light hand and dried her hair into an easy, tousled style.

Nick would bet twenty bucks Mike would never recognize this woman.

"Holy shit," he murmured.

She peered at herself in the mirror. "I've never been anything but a blonde. But I don't hate this color."

Clearly, that surprised her.

"It's—wow. You're beautiful. Then again, you'd look pretty if you were bald and wearing a garbage sack."

Sasha turned to him, hand on her hip. "I don't understand you. One minute, you're supportive, helpful, protective. The next you're an absolute bastard. Then you flip-flop again. When you say things like that... Are you just trying to confuse me?"

He could say yes. He could lie to her. But he saw the hurt on her face, the confusion. She'd been through so much, and the last thing she needed to be worrying about now was what the hell he thought or wanted or felt. And all right, he didn't like having her pissed off at him.

"The truth?"

She nodded. "That would be great."

"We're all better off if you don't like me. I have nothing for you but a stiff cock, and if Mike were here he'd do his best to beat my ass. I want you like hell. I always have, but it's easier if you hate me. Now that the jig is up, I'll stop being an asshole if you…" What? Try not to look so damn fuckable? It was up to him to control himself, not up to her to worry about his lust. "Keep your distance."

"And the sex I owe you for your 'fee?'"

Sure, he'd love that but… "Forget it. I would have helped you, regardless. It's the least I owed Mike for being a good friend. And I'll do everything in my power to make sure you and Harper have a safe, happy life."

Sasha cocked her head at him, looking both relieved and confused. "So…everything you said that night I arrived?"

He closed his eyes. "I questioned you about my loyalties to make you think. I didn't expect you to run from me. When I tackled you and got you under me…I wanted you too much to hide it for long. I knew you were afraid of me. I used my rape conviction to scare the shit out of you. Sorry. I should have just told you that unless you were looking for a lover, you shouldn't get too close to me. If you do, I'll seduce you."

"Because you just got out of prison and want an easy conquest." She sighed. "I feel so stupid."

"That's not entirely false. But it wouldn't be the whole truth, either." He tapped his thumb against his thigh, wondering how honest to be. Finally, he realized that besides not wanting to add to her stress, he hated her hating him. "The first time I saw you, you were sitting on that enclosed porch along the back of your house at dusk. Through the windows, I saw the sun light you up with a golden glow as you breastfed Harper, looking so peaceful. You were the most beautiful woman I'd ever seen. But there was something more about you. I saw your spirit. Your essence. Whatever you want to call it. You oozed kindness and goodness and an innocence that neither marriage nor childbirth could change. I wanted you—and I couldn't stop. I wanted to pleasure you, corrupt you, bask in you. I wanted to absorb whatever made you special. I wanted to learn to be better for you. I still do, and I'm probably doomed to failure. I knew then that if I hung around, my urge to claim you could zip past my friendship with Mike and wear down my self-control. I'm still sure that's true. But now that he's gone, the only thing stopping me is you."

Sasha looked dazed. "So you've just been pushing me away?"

When she looked as if she was really seeing him for the first time, he shrugged. "I'm good at being an asshole, so it came naturally."

"Last night, if I had asked you to make love to me…?"

"I'd still be deep inside you. Mike would be cursing me from above, and you'd hate yourself later. So let's drop it. Let's find Mike's evidence and get it into the right hands. Then your nightmare will be over."

Nick packed up all his gear, watching as she did the same. He was aware that she hadn't stopped staring at him. Shit. No matter how much he jacked off, she still made him hard. No matter how much he told himself not to look at her, every time he did, his heart flipped over. He'd lived for years off his gut instinct. It told him to go after her. But logic told him his instinct needed to shut the hell up.

"Done?" he asked as he zipped the last of his things into his backpack.

She closed her duffel. "Yes. Do you really think we'll find Mike's evidence? I have no idea what this key fits into."

At least she wasn't talking about his diarrhea of the mouth anymore. "That part is stumping me, too. I don't remember anything with a lock at the bandstand. Maybe he buried something. We'll look for whatever it is. Based on the size of the key, it's small."

"What happens if we don't find it?"

"We'll keep looking, and I'll make sure you and Harper stay safe." And he'd find new, creative ways to maintain distance between them or she'd wind up in his bed. "I'm not letting you die and I'm not giving up my revenge. You can bet on that."

She nodded solemnly.

He carried their bags to the SUV. She followed. The sun rose high. The warmth thinned as November pressed on. It would be Thanksgiving in a couple of weeks. It had never been his favorite time of year since an absent father and an overworked single mother trying to make ends meet in the 'hood hadn't left him much to be thankful for. Ditto for prison. Shit, he sounded like he was having a fucking pity party. He needed to put on his big-boy drawers and be grateful that Sasha had come to him for help. Getting revenge would make him damn thankful this year. So would letting her get on with a pretty, peaceful life.

They fell quiet as he dodged traffic toward the park. He donned his cap and slid the sunglasses on his face. She followed suit with her shades.

As disguises went, theirs were rudimentary—the best he could come up with on the fly. But this jaunt through the park should last a handful of minutes, so they didn't have to stay disguised very well or for very long.

Nick glanced her way. Her now-dark hair slid in silky waves over her shoulders, the sunlight catching the rich coffee skeins. She looked both bolder and somehow more delicate with the contrast of her dark hair against her fair skin.

He wanted her. Then again, he always did. He had to stop fixating and get practical.

After a drive-thru breakfast, they finally pulled onto Dreyfous Drive and took the winding road adjacent to the Museum of Art. They passed in front of the coffeehouse and parked in a spot closer to the bandstand.

As soon as they got out of the SUV, the wind picked up. The temperature had dropped discernably in the last thirty minutes. Cloud cover moved in. Winter weather was coming earlier than usual.

A quick glance told Nick that not many people lingered near the bandstand. The few moms pushing strollers were leaving before the chill got worse.

When Sasha shut her door, he locked the car and dragged in a bracing breath. Time to bring to light the evidence Mike had given his life to hide.

He headed to the walkway on the far side of the bandstand, away from the coffeehouse and the few people sitting at the tables with red umbrellas, clutching their hot brew and hurriedly eating beignets. Sasha followed, and he grabbed her hand, holding it in his. She gripped him like she was nervous.

"Relax. We're a couple out for a stroll. You've got the key around your neck?"

"Always." She breathed out, clearly searching for calm. "It's so different to be here now. The day I took my bridal pictures, it was spring. Sunny. Warm. It seemed like such a happy place. I remember being thrilled they had restored the bandstand so beautifully after Katrina. Today this place looks...ominous."

"Because you feel like you're being watched?"

"Yes."

Nick did, too. Maybe it was paranoia. No one seemed to be paying them any particular mind. A few stragglers loitered, some packing up lawn chairs since the day didn't look as promising as it had earlier. Joggers picked up pace to escape the wind as it kicked harder. More mothers with strollers disappeared to the parking lot. A photographer with a model wearing a decidedly springlike dress twirled in the wind, her teeth beginning to chatter. After another few shots, he tucked his equipment away and they left.

Sasha huddled close to Nick for warmth. "What do we do?"

They approached the bandstand. He wrapped an arm around her. To anyone else, he would appear a concerned lover shielding his woman from the cold. He took advantage of the pose and bent to her ear. "We look around for anything that might fit the key Mike left you."

She peered up as if glimpsing the bandstand for the first time. "I don't see anything at the top or bottom of the columns with a lock. Nothing in the roof structure. But they run electrical here."

He nodded. "At the bottom of the dome. It lights up at night."

"So there's an electrical box somewhere."

"Yep. I also see metal trash cans around the perimeter. And a bench over there."

"Yes. Mike could also have hidden something in the bushes. Or like you said, buried it."

True. "Any of those possibilities seem more likely to you? Some choice Mike might have gravitated to more than another?"

Sasha paused, studying the area again. "If he was protecting something under lock and key, I'm going to guess he was also shielding it from the elements and prying eyes. The bench is too open from beneath. Anyone picnicking or lying on the grass to dream up cloud formations could look over and see the underside."

"Yeah. And the trash cans get too much attention."

"From people using and emptying them. I agree. And the bushes would probably get trimmed too often to hide anything."

"Agreed. Katrina should have proven that burying anything in a swampy city below sea level is a bad idea," he drawled.

"When you put it like that, Mike wouldn't have buried whatever it is. I wasn't here when the hurricane hit, but Mike was devastated by all the damage. He loved this city."

"He did."

Mike had grown up in the best parts of the Big Easy. Nick had been intimately familiar with the worst and he'd hated it at times. But he couldn't deny it had given him good friends and a colorful adolescence. It had beat the hell out of spending every winter in the Jersey chill.

A passing jogger slowed as he approached the bandstand, seemingly to catch his breath. As he braced on his knees and dragged in air, he clapped eyes on them. Nick didn't know if the guy was simply staring at Sasha or up to no good. Either way, he wasn't taking chances. He lifted her chin and smiled her way. "We're being watched. Act like I've said something that makes you happy."

She lifted her lashes and met his stare. A grin flirted with her lips but her gaze looked so somber. "Do you think there's any chance we're going to succeed?"

"I'm betting my life on it." *Yours and Harper's, too.*

Her grin lifted into a warm smile, transforming her. Yeah, she was acting. But when the sun broke from the clouds to slant golden rays across her face, lighting her with a glow, her goodness shined through. She was a good mother. She'd been a good wife. She worked hard to be a good person. He'd bet she prided herself on that. Any man would be lucky to have Sasha. Hell, he'd count himself the most blessed man on the planet to spend even one night as her man.

He'd do anything to give her the chance to brighten the world for a lifetime.

Nick knew he should…but he couldn't resist the urge to dip his head and fit his lips across Sasha's, kissing her softly. He breathed her in. Gentle, delicately floral…with a bit of something spicy. Just like her.

When she might have pulled away, he cradled her face in both hands and stilled her. "A couple in love."

At his reminder, she stiffened. Ignoring that, he layered his mouth over hers again and caressed her face.

Little by little, she lost her starch, her posture softening, her lips gradually molding to his. Then he urged her open for him. Nick would have sworn he heard a soft female moan. Maybe it had been the wind. Or his wishful thinking. Either way, he swept inside and kissed her thoroughly until she clung to his shoulders and her breathing wasn't quite steady.

Only then did he pull back. "That's what I had in mind."

Her cheeks were rosy. "That was more kiss than necessary."

Nick checked the surrounding park. "Maybe not. The staring jogger is gone. So is most everyone else. Let's work fast."

"I'll explore the periphery, see if anything else seems worth searching."

"Do it like you're taking a stroll," he warned.

Sasha nodded. "I'll act wide-eyed and excited to be here."

Like it was her first trip. "Good. I'll keep an eye on you as I check out some of the fixed objects with passing curiosity."

As she unclasped her fingers from his with unhurried steps, his hand lingered. Truth was, he didn't want to stop touching her. And letting her out of his range bugged the control freak in him. But working fast and smart would do far more to make Sasha safe than refusing to let go.

Even after the last of his fingertips glided over her palm, he felt her touch burn through him as he strolled around the bandstand. Sasha wrapped her arms around herself as if she wished she had a coat—or needed his warmth.

Nick studied the stone steps, walked up, paced across the floor of the stone dome, then back down the other side. The electrical box stood maybe ten feet away.

When he reached it, he glanced down. Sure enough, the oblong gray panel had a door on the front, secured by a small lock. Nothing else he could see nearby opened with a key.

"Hey," he called out when Sasha drifted toward a nearby trash can. He held out his hand to her, and she strolled closer. "Did Mike have any friends who worked for the city? Someone who might have given him a key to this box?"

"We had a neighbor whose wife worked for the city. She and Mike talked fairly often about sites they loved and what it was like to work for local government. In fact, I think she worked for the city's parks and parkways department."

"Come here." He grabbed her hand and pulled her toward him. Their bodies collided. He dipped his head again, trying not to get lost in her sweetness as he unfastened the chain from her neck and let the key slide into his palm. Regretfully, he pulled away. "Let's see if your key fits this lock."

She sent a sideways glance at the panel. "Could we really have found it already?"

He shrugged. "It makes sense. I don't think Mike meant the search to be hard."

"But it was. He stumped me."

"He didn't explain everything because he didn't intend for you to dive into this dangerous shit alone."

Sasha frowned. "How was I supposed to know that?"

"He sent you the flowers with the card and the key. And he told you to find me, right?"

"Yes," she admitted as if the puzzle pieces suddenly fell into place. "You're right. He planned everything."

Nick nodded. "He meant for you to find his evidence with me."

In fact, the more Nick looked at the situation, he began to wonder if Mike had *wanted* him to take care of Sasha, not just now but always.

Nick pocketed her chain and palmed the key. His heart thudded as he sent her one last glance, then scrutinized the area. The coast was clear. He had the wind and the dropping temperature to thank. Who knew how long this boon would last?

He didn't waste another second before he bent to the hip-high box and shoved the key in the hole. It fit—but it didn't turn. The lock, like the door itself, had weathered with the elements. It was slightly rusted and stubborn, but with some brute force, it gave way. With a scrape and a squeak, it protested as it unlocked and the door slid ajar. Nick wrenched it the rest of the way. Beside him, Sasha gasped.

"What are we supposed to find?" she glanced up and down the electrical panel, scanning well-labeled breakers and a few plastic-coated wires. There wasn't much else to see.

"I don't know." He dragged out his phone and launched the flashlight app to make sure he wasn't missing anything hidden in the shadowed recesses of the box. With eager fingers, he tapped his way around the inside of the lid, the sides, the crannies underneath the guts of the panel. Nothing. Then he felt his way along the top.

His fingertips brushed over a hard, plastic ridge.

"I think I got something."

"What?"

Nick groped to find the best grip around the edges. A flash drive. He yanked it. The sounds of Velcro drifted up with the wind.

Just like that, he held Mike's evidence in his hand. Triumph and hope for Sasha's future roared through Nick. For the first time since receiving Mike's phone call asking him to look into Clifford because something seemed crooked, he had hope this situation might turn out right.

He shoved the drive and phone in his pocket, locked the panel door, and grabbed her hand. "Let's go."

Sasha clutched him tight as she scanned the park with wary eyes, as if she couldn't shake the feeling of being watched, either.

When they reached the car, he handed her back the chain and key. He didn't know how sentimental they might be for her. But damn it, he hated the thought that Sasha might be sitting right beside him and pining for Mike when some part of him wanted her to be his so damn badly he could barely stand it.

She slipped them back around her neck. "Now what?"

He pulled out of his parking spot and back onto the road. "We have to find some way to read what's on this drive. Make sure it's the evidence Mike meant to leave us." That time, weather, and human tampering hadn't erased it.

"Public libraries usually have computers anyone can use."

"We can't risk someone else getting a glimpse of whatever we've found, any virus zapping it, or any system administrator erasing it."

"You're right. Clifford is sneaky. He has eyes and ears everywhere."

Which was why Nick felt like, now that he had the flash drive, he was racing against the clock. It was only a matter of time before Clifford came after them. He didn't know how, when, or where; he just knew it was inevitable. He had to get the data to someone with enough power to take the DA down and get Sasha to safety.

Nick yanked his phone out of his pocket as he gunned the accelerator through a yellow light.

Xander picked up quickly. "You find it?"

Nick explained the situation. "I need a computer."

"You just left the park? Go west on Veterans Memorial. A few blocks beyond Division, you'll run into an electronics store on your left." He rattled off the address of the big chain's location. "I'll have something ready for you by the time you get there. You'll just have to haul inside and pick it up."

"Thanks." He frowned. "Are you tracking this SUV?"

"Yep." Xander sounded proud of himself. "GPS is my friend."

"You son of a bitch."

"Well, I'm a son of a bitch who's worried about you. Call me once you know what's on the flash drive. And tell Sasha that Harper is doing really well today. Her fever has broken."

"Will do." Nick hung up and focused on the road, looking beside and behind him to ensure no one followed them as he relayed the message about the girl.

Sasha breathed a sigh of relief. "Xander seems like a good friend."

"He and Javier are fantastic…now. Without London, I'm not sure either of them were going to make it much longer. Javier was quickly drinking himself to death after his first wife's murder, and Xander seemed well on his way to getting some flesh-eating STD."

"How did they wind up with the same woman?"

"Well, Xander and his brother weren't speaking at the time. London was working as Javier's secretary—and everyone knew he wanted her. So of course Xander was trying to seduce her. If the situation hadn't been so fucked up, it would have been funny."

"What I mean is that she's not legally married to them both, so—"

"No, she's legally married to Xander. Dulce is biologically Javier's daughter." He shrugged. "I don't know how they make it all work, but those three love each other. Whatever they share…it's what they all need. I've never seen either brother happier."

"If I hadn't seen them for myself, I would have doubted a successful relationship like that was possible. I certainly would have been wary about London's moral character." Sasha winced. "I grew up in a pretty religious household, and my dad would label their marriage blasphemy. But they really opened my eyes, and I'm so grateful for all they've done."

"Me, too." Nick waded his way through more lunchtime traffic until they reached the electronics store. He parked and yanked the keys from the ignition. "Let's go."

Three minutes later, they were walking out with a top-of-the-line MacBook Pro that would have no problem reading—and storing— whatever was on Mike's portable drive.

"Now what?"

Nick's thoughts raced. They'd checked out of the motel. But if this contained what he thought it did, they couldn't leave New Orleans without getting this fucking evidence to the FBI or the mayor—someone who could prosecute this wretched son of a bitch.

"You drive." He tossed her the keys and made his way around the vehicle. "This computer may have just enough battery life to read whatever Mike left us."

He tore the machine out of the box and booted it up as she left the parking lot. He skipped as much of the setup process as the operating system would allow, then shoved the flash drive into the port. One item popped up in the Finder window. When he clicked on it, the screen came to life.

Chapter Five

Sasha glanced from the road to the screen as it froze and a pop-up message about the operating system being out of date flashed, preventing Nick from playing the evidence.

"Fuck. Pull over," Nick commanded. "I'm not a typist and this is too hard to do in a moving car."

Sasha was cruising down the middle of three easterly lanes. "Anywhere in particular?"

"There." He pointed to the entrance of a parking lot to her right, leading to a Chipotle.

She changed lanes and did what he'd asked. The lot was starting to fill up, and she knew better than to park in the middle of the crowd, so she coasted around back, between two empty cars that probably belonged to employees, and put the SUV in park.

As she did, he turned on his hot spot and hooked it up to the computer. When the device prompted him to download more updates, he cursed and pressed the button to begin.

Over his cell signal, the download moved slowly.

"I wish we could play the video already," she said desperately.

"Yeah." He spoke the word as if he understood exactly how she felt, as if he'd waited and hoped like hell vengeance was coming.

Her impatience spiked. In moments, the mystery might be solved. The endless days and nights of misery might be over. Sadness that she'd lost Mike mixed with triumph that she and Nick could actually solve his murder. Mike would be so proud of her.

But Nick might be her biggest surprise. Despite being Mike's friend, she hadn't known him well. Nick had moved to Lafayette before she and Mike had begun dating. He'd been burying his mother the weekend she and Mike married, so she hadn't met him then, either. Their introduction after Harper's birth had been brief and oddly tense. So when Nick had acted like a predatory jerk in the last thirty-six hours, Sasha had remembered Mike's warnings and believed the worst.

Now that Nick had explained why he'd distanced himself and she had spent time in the circle of his protection and caring, she gauged him not by his words but through his actions. He could have slammed the door in her face that midnight she'd come, begging for help. He could have told her that he'd just gotten out of prison and didn't want any more problems with Walter Clifford. But he hadn't. He'd risked life, limb, and freedom to give her and Harper a tomorrow.

Equally telling, Nick was denying himself something he wanted badly—her. Apparently, he'd been doing it since the moment he set eyes on her. He could have taken advantage of her twenty times by now. After all, she'd agreed to be his mistress for a month, give him whatever kind of sexual payment he demanded. But, despite being without sex for over a year, he'd refused her body both times she'd offered it. Last night he'd bestowed dazzling pleasure on her without asking for anything in return. Instead, he had done his utmost to respect Mike's friendship and memory. Even now, he tried to protect her, especially from himself. His self-sacrifice struck her as both noble and sexy. Sasha didn't know everything he thought or felt, but deep down she knew he was a good man. No denying he aroused her body in ways she'd scarcely imagined.

Yes, he could be gruff and foul-mouthed and blunt. But he was also smart and protective—and so much more than the dangerous criminal she'd believed him to be days ago.

Circumstance. Situations. Inevitability. Fate. Whatever she called it, everything had led her to this moment with Nick. The day she'd buried Mike, she had felt as if she buried her heart with him. But here it was, fluttering in her chest with hope, respect, and desire—all for the man sitting beside her.

Oh, goodness. She was falling in love.

When had that happened?

Finally, another pop-up announced the completion of the operating system's update. He flipped back over to the video player and clicked the button. An image of Walter Clifford's office filled the screen. A little grainy, and the audio quality wasn't great. But Mike stood behind the desk, looking up nervously at the camera.

Sasha gasped. It was hard to look at her late husband—his familiar movements and mannerisms. That face she'd know anywhere. The cowlick at the front of his pale hair. The remnants of the sunburn he'd gotten after washing their cars without putting on sunscreen the previous weekend.

"I'll be goddamned. Mike…buddy." Nick sounded choked up.

Sasha stifled tears and reached for his hand. "It's him. Oh, my gracious. What is he doing?"

"Inexpertly setting up a hidden camera in his boss's office. Damn it, Mike. Why didn't you ask me to wire that place for you?"

"Maybe everything happened too fast?"

"Probably. And because the one time I visited your house, he noticed I couldn't stop staring at you." Nick looked sheepish. "I'm so damn sorry I wasn't there."

"Look at the date stamp." She caught sight of it in the bottom right corner, a number that faded in, flashed a few times, then dwindled away. "Wasn't that the day after you got arrested?"

Nick squinted at the numbers, then nodded. "It fucking is. He must have known that installing surveillance in Clifford's office was dangerous. I got out two days later." After the police had magically forgotten to allow him a phone call, and the Santiagos had come looking for him. Money talked, and theirs had helped him make bail quickly. "I would have handled it."

By then, Mike's fate had likely been sealed.

Sasha wasn't even sure what to feel. Angry? Regretful? In the end, she settled for somewhere between sad and resigned since she couldn't change the past. She could only move on from here. She would always miss her sweet, salt-of-the-earth husband.

But she was beginning to believe Nick Navarro might be her future.

Suddenly, Mike jolted and shoved something into a drawer, then hastily shut it before darting around the desk and heading toward the camera—and the office door. His footsteps sounded loud. As he crept closer to the camera, it picked up a sheen of sweat on his face and the nervous shift in his eyes.

"Damn it," Nick murmured. "But this is my thing. He sucked at clandestine."

She couldn't disagree. Had the honesty she'd treasured in Mike been one of the qualities that led to his demise?

"Porter. What are you doing here?" said a faint voice belonging to someone out of the camera's view. But Sasha knew exactly who it belonged to. She'd heard Walter Clifford speak too often not to recognize his gruff tones.

"Looking for you. I wanted to give you an update on the Ector case."

"Later." Clifford sounded dismissive. "I just came back from lunch, and I'm late for a conference call. See me at four."

"Of course." Mike all but bowed and scraped as he headed for the door.

Watching him leave the screen cramped Sasha's stomach with a physical pain. He disappeared from the shot quickly, and it felt like losing him all over again. There would be no more of Mike's movements or smiles or complaints on a Sunday morning that the most important political shows shouldn't be airing when people should be in church. She wouldn't see him rock his daughter, touch his smooth cheek, or hear him sing in the shower ever again.

He was simply gone.

"Shit," Nick muttered beside her.

Sasha refocused on the screen and watched Clifford shuffle into view. Balding, portly, pushing sixty, he looked far more like someone's grouchy grandfather than a corrupt politician and criminal mastermind. The man scowled and searched the room, seemingly suspicious, before he shook his head, plopped down behind his desk, and yanked the receiver of his phone to his ear.

Seconds later, he began hissing at whomever was on the other line. "Has Mike Porter been sneaking around your office?" After a pause, Clifford gripped the phone tighter. "Well, today is the third time I've found him snooping around mine. I don't like it. I'm pretty sure he overheard us fixing the evidence in that criminal dumping case against that fucking oil driller. The moral stick up that church boy's ass has become an antenna, and I haven't been able to redirect him." Again, another hesitation while the other party—probably a sheriff or police chief—spoke. "Fuck the money. We stand to lose our reputations and careers if Porter has evidence and he goes public." Clifford swore. "Let me find out what he knows. If he's onto us, I'll make sure he can't talk anymore."

Beside her, Nick stiffened. And he looked at the screen like he hated Walter Clifford almost more than he could contain, like he had to swallow it down to keep it from spewing out, like he had to breathe through it or he might explode. Sasha understood that. The same furious incredulity spread through her. How dare that man leave a woman without her husband, a child without her father, a friend without his buddy? But he'd talked about murder so casually, so thoughtlessly—as if he'd done it before.

After another hesitation during which the cop must have mentioned another problem, the DA scowled. "Yeah? Keep that fucking P.I. Navarro in jail until we can figure out what he knows about my affairs. And for fuck's sake, don't tell the press who's accused him of rape. They'll start connecting the dots, and the whole thing will turn into a PR nightmare. My niece will crumble under the pressure. Fiona is a pretty girl...but not a bright one. We'll get this fucker's case rammed through fast. Find out who Navarro's attorney is and put the screws to him. Make sure Judge Marburn presides when it gets to trial. He owes me. Don't fuck this up."

Sasha watched Nick, glanced at the screen for a moment, then back to the seething, dangerous man beside her again. Not only had Mike captured the evidence that might put away his murderer, he had also proven that Nick really had been framed.

His jaw clenched. He didn't say anything for a moment, like he was too furious to speak without giving into his violent urge to kill Walter Clifford.

She lay a gentle hand on his forearm, trying to ease his tension. "We've got him. This should be enough to send him to prison for a long time."

"You better fucking believe it. We need to figure out who to give this to. Who will make sure this evidence gets into the hands of someone with enough power to take Clifford down? Since he's the one responsible for prosecuting crime in this parish, it won't be simple. And you can bet he won't prosecute himself. New Orleans isn't my town, so I don't know who to trust."

"I've been thinking..." She gnawed on her lip and thought the idea through. It was risky, but doing nothing was deadly. "Make a copy of this on the hard drive. We need a backup."

"Already done, and as soon as we hit some reasonably secure Wi-Fi,

I'll be sending it to the Santiago brothers for safekeeping. Their backup system is incredibly hack-proof, fireproof, and redundant. Now what?"

Sasha had never seen Nick any way except sure of himself and his direction. When she looked back, he'd done so much to help her, make sure she had a future. What if she could expunge his record and give them both the vengeance they sought? What if she could give him a happy future, too?

"Mike had this coworker Josh. He's a sweet guy. A real crusader. He once got into hot water at work for listening to a defendant's side of the story and wanting to drop all charges. In the end, Josh was right, the guy Clifford wanted to charge with the crime was innocent. I remember Mike coming home and shaking his head because their slimeball boss didn't care that he might send an innocent man to prison. Clifford only cared that the police had no other suspects, so without this slam-dunk trial, his conviction rate didn't look as dazzling."

"Yeah." Nick snorted. "No one knows better than me that he's got a hard-on for sending the innocent up river. So this Josh guy can help?"

"I think so. After that incident, the mayor put him on a citywide crime task force. From what I can tell, he made a lot of high-powered friends. I'm betting if we contact Josh he can put us in touch with the right people. I mean, Josh and these folks went over Clifford's head once. Why wouldn't they do it again?"

Nick hesitated for a moment, then nodded, the gesture gaining strength the more he thought about it. "Yeah. You know how to reach Josh?"

"I think so. Let me double-check with some Internet searches."

He thrust the computer in her direction. "Be quick. The laptop battery is dying. We need to plug this thing in."

"Where? We checked out of our motel."

"I'll hunt down another one." He grabbed his phone. "You find Josh."

For a few silent minutes, they both scoured their respective devices. It didn't take long to find *Krandall, Joshua*. She found a home address, no phone number. Of course, it was midday Monday, so he would likely be at the office. How could she reach him under Clifford's nose?

"Got one," Nick burst into the silence. "I found a motel right off Highway 61, not too far from the DA's office. It's a dive, not affiliated with a chain. Their website says they'll take cash."

Sasha conveyed her findings about Josh. "We might have to call his office and arrange something this evening."

"Too risky. It's damn likely all calls in and out of the DA's office are recorded."

Nick was right. "Then we may have to wait until he gets off work and drop by his house."

At first, Nick scowled at the delay, but Sasha watched his thoughts working as he seemingly considered all their choices and possible outcomes. "All right. That gives us time to grab some more ammo and prep a game plan for approaching this guy. And a nap. I barely slept a fucking wink last night."

Sasha hated to hear that. "Insomnia?"

Nick slanted a glance at her that silently asked if she was serious. "I can't sleep next to you when I'd rather be inside you."

She felt heat crawl up her cheeks...and swirl between her legs.

Of course he hadn't rested. She'd had an amazing orgasm. And he hadn't. No, that wasn't quite true. He had given her a mammoth, earth-shaking, jaw-dropping, scream-worthy, life-changing cataclysm of pleasure. Then she'd allowed him to goad her into anger, and all thought of throwing herself at him again had fled.

Sasha felt more than vaguely guilty. She wished she'd given him pleasure in return instead.

"Then I'll give you some space so you can rest. If you don't mind, I'd like to drive by Josh's place first, make sure he really still lives there. He'd actually just purchased a house shortly before Mike's death, so chances are good but..."

"Let's go." Nick took the computer back from her hands as she navigated the traffic to Mid-City.

Thankfully, she didn't need the GPS on his phone to remember Josh's location. She and Mike had come here, hand in hand, to mingle with friends and celebrate new beginnings. Had that been a mere two years ago?

Sasha stopped in front of the starter home. It was long on charm, with brick steps, craftsman pillars, a wide porch, and what appeared to be original stained glass in the transom above the front door. However, the cottage was short on space, looking dwarfed by much bigger neighbors on either side. But it had been freshly painted, was well maintained, and had original hardwoods inside, as she recalled.

Nick sidled out of the SUV and opened the mailbox at the curb. "Empty."

He headed to the side yard. Tucked against the fence, adjacent to the patchy concrete driveway, sat a huge plastic trash can and a recycle bin. He pretended to trip over the bin, nudging the lid off the squatty receptacle and spilling out most of the contents.

"What are you doing?" Sasha frowned.

"Double-checking." He glanced around to ensure none of the neighbors were being nosy. But in this neighborhood, people worked. It seemed unlikely that anyone would be watering the flowers on their porch or taking their dog for a walk right now.

Sasha believed in respecting others' privacy. She totally valued hers. But locating Josh quickly and quietly could well be life or death. "Find anything?"

After he bent to tuck away the newspapers and the empty, rinsed milk carton, he did an amazing imitation of someone picking up flyers, ads, and discarded envelopes without actually reading a word.

"Bingo. He still lives here. He tossed the water bill, presumably after he paid it, into the recycle bin." Nick shook his head as if Josh had made a critical mistake.

Despite the tense situation, Sasha had to laugh. "He didn't shred, so off with his head."

The smile that spread across Nick's full lips took her breath away. White teeth flashed against his olive complexion. His dark eyes sparked with something both funny and alive. He almost looked…happy. It was a breath-stealing sight.

"Okay, maybe not that severe but I believe in being careful. Identity theft is serious business. Why make those fuckers' crimes easier?"

"You're right." She helped him put the last of the paper back into the bin. "So we'll come back later?"

Before they could answer that question, a pretty redhead stepped out the front door, with a little white furball on a leash. She glanced warily at Nick. "Can I help you?"

Sasha stepped forward. "Are you Josh's"—she looked at the woman's bare left hand—"girlfriend?"

She shook her head, the ginger strands of her quirky bob swaying. "No. His dog walker. I'm Hannah. This is Monster."

When the six-pound pup barked in a tone Sasha was sure he meant to be menacing, she tried not to smile.

Hannah laughed on her behalf. "Ferocious, huh? Are you friends of Josh's?"

"We are." Nick took her hand. "My girlfriend and I rolled into town late last night. We're staying a few days and we'd like to visit him. Will he be home tonight?"

The dog walker looked Nick's way, then stepped back, as if suddenly put off by his size or intensity. "I don't know. I only walk his dog. I'll tell him you're in town. What are your names?"

Nick managed a false wince of regret. "I wish you wouldn't. We really want to surprise him. We haven't seen him since his housewarming party."

"That's right." Sasha nodded to ease the woman's suspicions. "Shortly after he made that task force at the DA's office, right?"

"Exactly." Nick sounded as if he knew that for a fact.

The details helped smooth the woman's skeptical expression. "Oh, it has been a long time since you've seen him. Okay, I won't mention it. He should be home around six."

"Perfect. Thanks for your help." Sasha smiled, then reached out to the dog. "Bye, Monster. Cute little guy."

The canine barked happily and allowed her to pet his head, then swiped his affectionate tongue over her wrist.

Hannah eased back. "Have a great day."

With a wave, they jaunted back to the SUV, then headed to a strip mall that had both a sporting goods store and an electronics boutique. Errands managed, they went to the motel Nick had scouted out. It had a colonial facade and a traditional brick-and-shutters front, along with an air of glory days long past.

"I'm sorry it's a shithole," he murmured beside her as they parked.

She shrugged. "It's a bed and a shower. I've gone days—sometimes weeks—without either. I'm grateful."

His face tightened with something that looked an awful lot like regret. "We're going to nail Clifford so you never have to go without either again."

She believed he would do anything to make that happen. He was the kind of man who kept his word. He had even gone to prison to keep a promise to Mike.

They exited with their purchases and luggage, then entered a sad lobby with brown floors and a big fleur-de-lis affixed to the front of the check-in desk. An old man who couldn't have acted more bored checked them in. Up a narrow stairwell, past a broken light fixture, then down a hall with green turf open to a dingy pool atrium below, they found room 218.

Nick shoved the key in the cinnamon-colored door with rusting accents. Inside, the burgundy-and-beige-patterned carpet didn't quite hide the stains. Same with the brown bedspread splashed with red, blue, green, and pink blobs that might have once been flowers. A musty, moldy odor wafted from the air vents and blended with the stench of cigarette smoke.

"Jesus, this place is worse than I thought." Nick grimaced.

It was, but that wasn't really Sasha's concern right now.

The big blue numbers on the nightstand's cheap digital clock read five minutes after two. They had four hours to wait. As antsy as she felt, how could she kill the time?

A glance at Nick gave her ideas that made her body flash hot.

He unloaded their luggage and purchases onto a desk shoved in the corner and frowned. "I'm fucking beat." He lowered the spread on the king-size bed, then sat and doffed his boots. "Let's get this video copied so we have backups. Then we can grab some shut-eye."

"Are you going to e-mail one to the Santiagos?"

He grabbed the computer, plugged it into the outlet, and connected to the Internet signal. "Not on this hotel's Wi-Fi. It's not secure. Getting on the network didn't even require a password. I'll send the evidence using my hot spot."

The file took a while to send, but it finished and he closed the laptop's lid. "Done."

"So the evidence is safe?"

He nodded. "Clifford can't squirm away now."

Sasha closed her eyes in relief. This violent, tragic period in her life might really be over. She wanted Mike's killer punished so she could finally live again. It seemed so surreal that after fifteen months of fear, danger, and near death, this nightmare might be over in four short hours.

Where would she and Harper go then? Where would they settle down? What would they do with the rest of their lives? How would she feel when she didn't have to spend her every waking moment with Nick?

Empty. She didn't want to live without him.

"Wake me in an hour," he insisted.

"All right."

"Thanks." He tugged off his shirt.

With the fabric gone, Nick exposed tribal tattoos that swept up his lean ribs on one side, covered his bulging pectoral, drifted around his solid shoulder before changing direction to cascade down his rippling biceps and thick forearm. Sasha tried not to swallow her tongue as he lay on one side of the bed, closest to the door, and his body stilled.

In seconds, he dropped off. His deep, even breathing was barely audible in the room. And she was still staring at him, dazed by the sight of his wide back bunched and defined with more muscle.

Goodness, Nick Navarro was a beautiful man.

He wasn't Mike. No one was. But she'd loved her late husband the way a girl cherished Prince Charming. She'd given her heart to him in a sugary drop, fallen with him into a champagne bubble of warmth and comfort. His death had burst that. With the pretty pink bow of forever ripped away, Sasha had been forced to push through thorns and become a woman.

Her sweet prince would never ride up on his white horse to save her because the villain had killed him. But the big, dark Beast beside her now would vanquish the demon, with her at his side. And she would fight to the death to protect her child—and her future with Nick.

There was nothing soft or sweet or innocent about the way she wanted him. She ached for him desperately, urgently, passionately. He challenged her between the ears, roused the flesh between her legs, and ignited a blaze between her ribs she knew would burn eternally.

Asking how or why was a stupid waste of time. Mike's murder had proved that no one was guaranteed a tomorrow. She was going to wring every moment—and experience—she could from her time with Nick. She was going to tell him what was in her head and her heart. If he didn't want her for more than a night…well, she would at least have the satisfaction of knowing she had given herself completely and honestly.

Suddenly, as if he sensed her gaze—or her decision—his eyes flashed open. Sasha found herself freefalling into his relentless stare, which seemed to remove every stitch from her body, despite the fact he wasn't touching her at all.

"Nick?" She heard the breathlessness of her own voice.

"I need a shower," he growled as he bounded off the bed and nearly ran to the bathroom, slamming the door behind him.

Sasha frowned. He was…so jumpy. Tense. Wound up.

Sexually frustrated?

Suddenly, all the showers he took—morning and night—made sense. He wasn't a clean freak or a germophobe. If he had been, they certainly wouldn't be staying in this dive of a motel. He was masturbating in the shower to curtail his desire so he wouldn't jump on her like the ravenous Beast she suspected he could be.

Like she wanted him to be.

It was up to her to prove she could not only handle that animal part of him, but that she craved it.

They still had hours to kill before they could return to Josh's place, so now was the perfect time to show Nick exactly the woman she'd become.

His woman.

* * * *

Son of a bitch. Nick yanked on the tap and jerked off his jeans. He unwrapped the toy-sized bar of soap resting in the dish in the stall, then stepped under the weak spray.

He had to spend another night beside Sasha, sharing her sheets, wrapped in her sweetly female scent. How the fuck was he going to stop himself from stripping off every stitch she wore, baring all her sugar-soft skin to his greedy gaze, then crawling between her legs to shove his way home? Because that's how he thought of her now. His person. His woman. His home. With her was where he belonged.

Jacking off wasn't a substitute for her anymore, and he swore he'd lose his goddamn mind if he couldn't touch her, taste her flavor on his tongue, and feel her every limb and orifice cling to him soon.

He could lie to himself, but why bother? He didn't just want her because he hadn't had sex with a woman in well over a year. He didn't burn for her because she was beautiful. He coveted her because she was good and warm and giving. She was his sun and lit his darkness with so much light. Now that he'd seen the fierce survivor and protector in her, he only hungered for Sasha more.

Last night, she'd looked about as eager to take him deep inside her as she was to catch a disease. So where did that leave him?

Utterly fucked. No. Fucking his hand for relief. Again.

Nick lathered the harsh soap in his hands, which smelled faintly of artificial coconut and chemicals. He tried to block the crappy scent out as he tossed the small bar into the dish, then grabbed his throbbing cock.

He had to end the danger to Sasha tonight. He had to make certain they were safe—for Mike, for her daughter, for his own freaking sanity. Then he'd start over, maybe take Javier and Xander up on their offer, see if Sasha could picture any sort of future with him. If not, he'd find someone else he'd want eventually, right? Someday…maybe. On the twelfth of never. After hell froze over.

As fixated as he felt on Sasha Porter right now, he doubted he would ever feel a shred of desire for any other woman.

Pushing the thought aside, he tried to focus on the sensation of his soapy hand gliding down his sensitive shaft, then roughing his way up to the head, which he caressed with his roving thumb. He imagined Sasha touching him, arousing him. Tingles streaked and blistered through his veins. Excitement clawed through his system. His cock jerked in his grip.

Yeah, orgasm wasn't going to take long. But he was quickly finding that wasn't synonymous with satisfaction. If anything, he felt emptier beside Sasha when he'd just given himself temporary, hollow relief.

But it was safer than not controlling his raging need at all.

A click sounded above the din of the water. Nick paused mid-stroke. The squeak of the door filled the little bathroom next. The rush of cool air disrupted the steam swirling around him.

His heart stopped. The only person in the room with him was Sasha, and no way she would voluntarily come into the bathroom while he was wet and naked and wanting her.

Had Clifford's goons found them already? Come to kill them?

Anxiety iced through him as he rinsed his hands and leaned to his left to peer around the shower curtain. He had to know his enemy, how many, how armed. If he survived, he'd curse himself for the carelessness of leaving his weapon on the nightstand. Would Sasha see it? Use it to save herself?

Or was it already too late?

Shifting his weight a bit more, he'd just visually cleared the edge of the shower curtain when he heard the sweetest, sultriest sound.

"Nick?" Sasha. She sounded jittery…but not afraid.

Maybe they weren't under attack. But something had happened to prod her into the shower with him.

"What? You okay?" he asked, then pulled back the cheap plastic curtain enough to expose his face and clap eyes on her. His breath—and his heart—stopped.

She was utterly, head-to-toe naked. She met his gaze with hazel eyes full of resolution. And need.

Sasha Porter wanted him. She didn't even have to say the words. He saw it on her face.

For a long moment, Nick couldn't do anything except stare. And ache. And marvel that she was the most beautiful woman he'd ever seen without a stitch.

Her long hair, now dark, fluttered over the smooth skin of her slender shoulders, onto the swells of her naturally heavy breasts. They were tipped with delicate rosy nipples that stood ready for his lips to suck and tease. She tapered into a small waist and a flat belly, which soon gave way to the flare of her womanly hips and generous, creamy thighs. As a natural blond, she had a faint dusting of fair hair shielding her pussy. He imagined her wet and pink, legs spread, waiting just for him.

Her hands fluttered nervously to the scar bisecting her between the hip bones. A couple of faint silvery lines shot up around the point of incision, now mostly faded. "I'm not perfect."

"You are to me."

She smiled faintly and pressed on as if he hadn't spoken. "But I'm hoping you'd rather have the pleasure we could share together than whatever you could give yourself…"

So she'd figured out what he did in the shower, huh?

"Always." His heart hammered. "You offering?"

"Yes."

"Because you owe me?" God, he didn't want her to say that. If she did… He gritted his teeth, fearing he might lose his fucking mind. He'd have to turn her away again.

She shook her head. "Because I'm falling in love with you."

Her words went straight to his cock. He hadn't thought he could get harder. Nick was shocked to find out that he, in fact, totally could.

God, he couldn't touch her quick enough, couldn't reach her soft body fast enough. He cut off the water and grabbed a towel off the rack. With one hand, he rubbed at the droplets beading over his skin. With the other, he curled his fingers around her arm and brought her close.

"Be sure."

"That I want you? I am."

"That you love me. I fell for you the moment I saw you. That might sound dumb, but…there it is. If you agree to be mine now, I won't give you up. You'll stay mine."

Sasha didn't hesitate. She didn't shake her head or frown, back away in objection, or tell him to pound his own cock again. She didn't do or say any of the fifty things he'd imagined she might if he admitted how he felt.

Instead, she softened, her lips lifting in a gentle, reassuring smile. "You're mine, too."

He dragged the towel over his middle one last time, then tossed it on the basin. "Absolutely, baby. Totally, utterly yours."

"Good." She lifted her hand to him, and he realized her fingers trembled.

Nick stepped from the stall and took her hand in his. "You're nervous. Unsure?"

"Worried," she countered. "I don't have a lot of experience, and I want to please you."

"Just breathe and say yes. You don't have to do any more than that to thrill me. And relax. I don't want you afraid of me."

"I'm not." She shook her head, sending her hair tumbling softly. "You'll never hurt me, just make me feel good in ways that will blow my mind completely. I hope I can do the same for you." She fell quiet. "But I have to say one other thing… If you're worried about Mike, I think he would have approved. After all, he threw us together."

Nick was relieved she'd come to the same realization he had. "Yeah. He knew how much I wanted you. I wasn't good at hiding it."

"I had no idea."

"Oh, he did. About five minutes after he introduced us, he warned me away. My attraction for you was all over my face, so Mike dragged me out to the yard and confronted me."

"What did he do, threaten to…beat you up?" She frowned. "That doesn't sound like Mike."

No, his pal hadn't been one for violence. "He said if I crossed the line with you that he and I would no longer be friends."

And given how long they'd been close, Nick had known Mike meant that.

Sasha gasped. She understood the gravity of the threat, too. "So you stayed away—literally—for the rest of his life. Heavens… All through dinner that night, I thought you were detached, almost disinterested."

He shook his head. "I honored my promise to Mike. I kept my distance."

"But in his final hours, he ensured we'd be together again."

"Yeah. And now I want you so bad I can't fucking stand another moment without touching you." He stepped closer, then bent to whisper in her ear. "I intend to make you wet, make you scream. Make you mine."

She shuddered against him. "Please."

"I'm going to love being inside you." He picked her up, fitting his hands under her lush, firm ass, and slanted his face to hers. "Kiss me."

Sasha didn't hesitate, just wrapped her arms around his neck, her legs around his waist, and parted her pretty bow lips to him.

As Nick carried her out of the bathroom, he barged into her mouth and sought out all the sweetest recesses. As he tasted her, he approached the bed and dropped her onto the starched white sheets.

With one arm thrown above her head and the other tossed out beside her, Sasha wasn't hiding any part of herself from him. She wasn't even trying. Instead, she wriggled her hips as if seeking relief from the ache she couldn't deny. Her back arched as she dragged in a breath and implored him silently with half-parted lips and a sensual stare.

Nick wanted to savor her, but urgency crushed his self-control. He lowered himself on top of her, covering her body with his own, and plowed between her delicate lips again, swallowing her gasp.

Shit. He should slow down.

Just one more second... But he felt like he wouldn't be able to breathe again until he had more of her flavor on his tongue, her silken skin under his fingers.

Since the first moment he'd laid eyes on her nearly three years ago, he'd burned to hold her. When he'd sat in a cell for interminable months, he'd shelved his guilt and fantasized that one day he'd be free to tug Sasha beneath him and devour her with all the hunger raging through his body. In his mind, he'd made love to her hundreds of times. He'd brought her to climax over and over with screaming, strangled cries in every way known to man.

Until today, Sasha hadn't really considered him her lover.

Nick jerked his lips from hers, panting hard. "You okay?"

"Of course. You won't break me."

He slanted a glance at her. "As badly as I want to fuck you, I might."

A blush stole up her cheeks. "You talk too much."

"You saying I should be getting busy with you instead?" He laughed.

She peppered kisses up his neck, along his jawline, and slanted her mouth under his. "Exactly."

The woman surprised him all the time, and god, he loved that about her.

"Oh, baby. The next sounds in this room will be you screaming for me."

A smile flitted across her lips before she hooked her arms around his neck and lifted herself to him, breasts pressed to his chest. He took her mouth.

Fuck, he could taste the love in her kiss. She'd only ever given herself to the man she had married. But she was surrendering to him now. Devotion flowed from her fingertips. Acceptance oozed from her soft palms, gliding onto his skin. She believed in him. Wanted him. Opened her heart to him.

Nick intended to make sure she spent forever with him.

Sasha's fingertips whispered down the line of his spine before she cupped his ass and lifted her hips to him in a blatant invitation no man could misunderstand. He started to sweat.

Fuck taking things slow. That's what next time was for.

"Sasha," he groaned.

"I want you." She looked into his eyes, hers so hazel-green and pleading.

"I want you, too, baby. I just need a condom." And fuck if it wasn't going to kill him to break away from her for even an instant for a dumbass piece of latex.

Wrenching up from the mattress, Nick found the box and tore into it, quickly ripping a foil square and rolling the slippery casing over his cock. The instant he finished, he launched himself back on top of her and captured her mouth again.

Beneath him, she whimpered and opened in welcome, knees bending to surround his hips. She poured her soul into the touch of her fingers and tangle of their tongues. "Hurry."

His dick sure wanted him to, but he'd waited way too long for this woman to simply shove his way inside her and pound out an orgasm.

"As soon as we make a few things clear." Because there was no way she was slipping through his fingers.

"What?" she sounded impatient. "You want to be in charge in bed."

"Always. But that's not—" He sighed. Damn, he needed to spit the words out. If she was going to argue…well, he knew how to coax her and change her fucking mind. Besides, he wasn't asking. Sasha was his, and he wouldn't take no for an answer. "Once we eliminate Clifford, you're marrying me. I know my past looks bad on paper but—"

"Yes."

No arguments? "Really? You mean that?"

"You and I know well that life can be short. I love you. I'm sure. Why wait? Besides, little girls should have a strong father figure in their lives. Harper needs you to be hers. Mike chose you to take his place in my life. I'm sure he'd want you to help me raise Harper, too."

Nick didn't really get warm fuzzies much. But…damn it. Everything Sasha said filled him with a flurry. "You're right. I'll always watch over Harper, protect her. She needs siblings, too."

"You want more children?"

"Fuck, yeah." The thought of her belly swelling with the child he'd put inside there nearly undid him. "With you. Baby…I can't wait."

Sasha spread her legs wider. "Then don't."

"Yeah. Hold on." It had been a long time for both of them. "This is going to be a rough ride."

She sighed his name as if that didn't upset her in the least and clutched his shoulders.

Gripping her hips, he dipped his head and nipped his way across her neck and the swells of her breasts—he'd come back here later—then probed her opening.

His head slid through her folds like butter. She was slick and tight and as close to heaven as he'd ever been.

She squeezed his arms in a passion-filled grip, as if braced for pleasure.

Nick held her tighter and breathed his way deeper inside her pussy.

As he did, she let a high-pitched cry loose from her throat.

He jerked his hips, stroking, desperate, on fucking fire to bury every inch inside her.

She clenched her thighs around his hips and urged him on even more.

He goddamn gave her everything, surging into her with a push and a rush until he couldn't shove his way in any further.

She cried out, voice hoarse, fingernails embedding in his skin, perspiration covering her as he unleashed his desire and made her his.

With stroke after hard stroke, the bed squeaked. He wrenched gasps and moans from her lips. Bliss streaked fire through his body.

Jesus, he wasn't going to last. It had been forever since he'd had sex, and he had never wanted a woman as fiercely as he wanted this one. Whatever he felt tearing through his veins and decimating his restraint wasn't mere desire. This was unraveling his brain, changing the way he perceived ecstasy. It was rewriting his definition of pleasure.

Beneath him, she tightened—her grip around his shoulders, her legs around his hips, and her sweet pussy all over his weeping cock.

Fuck, he needed her to come with him now.

Nick reached a thumb between them and dragged it over her clit. Her harsh breaths stuttered. She tossed her head back and forth. Her little pearl hardened beneath his touch.

"No…"

"Yeah, baby. You fucking come for me now."

"It's…so…"

"Good? Let it go. Fucking scream it."

She tensed, her body arched, her rosy little mouth bowed into an *O*. And she wailed his name at the top of her lungs as she spasmed, clenched, and climaxed with her entire body.

Nick knew that would never get old for him.

It was the last thought he had before the pleasure steamrolled him and he lost his damn mind, emptying himself into her as she undid him and took hold of his heart forever.

Into the silence punctuated only by their panting, he clutched her tight.

"What was that?" She sounded as stunned as he felt.

"Not just sex." He knew the difference. Nick was pretty sure what they'd just shared had unraveled his brain, rewired him for her and her alone, and remade him into a committed man. "But next time will be better."

"How?" Her gaze was stunned, as if she couldn't even think of a way their sex could remotely improve.

He grinned. "I'll be slower. I'll have more control, I promise."

"Why bother?" She sighed. "That was so damn amazing."

He'd never once heard her swear. Hearing her so emphatic now made him laugh. "How about if I promise it will be someplace nicer?"

Sasha grimaced. "That, I would love."

"You got it, baby. You've got me. Always. I love you."

"As crazy as it sounds, I love you too, Nick. Let's catch a bad guy and live happily ever after."

He didn't think Walter Clifford intended to make things quite that easy, but he didn't want to worry Sasha, so he just nodded. "Absolutely."

Chapter Six

Nick lay staring at the stained ceiling, absently stroking Sasha's back as she curled against him like a kitten, soft and all but purring. The thought made him smile. Sex the second time had been even better than the first. He'd dragged out her pleasure, made her wait and claw and beg for it. Then she'd undone him with a talented tongue and her bedroom eyes until he'd shoved her on her back again and ridden her to a euphoric climax that still had him reeling.

He could handle fifty years of that with her.

First, they had to dispose of Walter Clifford. A glance at the clock told Nick that he and Sasha needed to be out the door to reach Josh Krandall's house in about forty minutes.

Had they really been making love for the last three hours? As boneless as his legs felt, he believed that.

The cell phone buzzing on his nightstand broke into his thoughts. Nick snatched it up before the sound woke Sasha. "What?"

"Oh, grouchy. You're either not getting any or I interrupted," Xander teased.

"Neither." Nick eased away from Sasha and headed to the desk, speaking in low tones. "You calling for a reason or just want to yank my chain?"

The younger Santiago sighed. "As much as I love to rile you, this isn't a social call."

Something about the way he said those words made Nick suddenly wish it was. "Harper?"

"She's fine. But we've moved to a safe house the Edgington brothers have just to be certain."

His gut tightened. "What happened?"

"Someone broke into your rental a few hours ago. They trashed the place but didn't take anything."

"Coincidence?" But even as the question left Nick's mouth, he shook his head. No way he was buying that.

"What are the odds? I think they were looking for something."

"The video. It's reasonable to assume Clifford knows we have it." Nick wasn't sure how the asshole managed to work that fast, but he was ruthless and had power. And he was getting frantic—almost reckless—to find Sasha before Mike's evidence leaked out.

"That's my guess. One other thing you should know. They left graffiti on the walls that read *YOU'RE GOING TO DIE, BITCH.*"

Nick's heart stopped cold.

"Fuck." He looked over his shoulder to find Sasha still sleeping. "So Clifford also knows she's with me."

"Yeah. You need to wrap this up fast. If this DA already linked the house we rented to you, it won't be long before they come sniffing around for Harper."

Which also put London and Dulce in danger. Damn it.

"I'll take care of it tonight. I've got to go."

"Damn it, Nick. I know that tone," Xander shouted. "Tell me your game plan. Don't do anything stupid."

Stupid? No. Just whatever was necessary to keep Sasha and Harper safe. "I'll call you in a few hours."

"Nick—"

He hung up. With his gut screaming at him, he lifted the laptop lid, clicking onto a local TV station for all the latest New Orleans news. There at the top, just as he feared, was a developing story. *ADA Murdered At Stoplight In Broad Daylight.*

Josh Krandall was dead.

Clifford wasn't fucking around. The asshole had been tracking them most of the day. Nick realized the fucker must not know where they'd holed up now or he'd already be beating on their motel room door. But by cutting down the people who could help Nick, the bastard was sending a message.

Too bad for him Nick wasn't listening. He intended to make the dirty DA pay for everything he'd done.

Nick mentally rolled through all his options. Going to the cops or the FBI was no bueno. Clifford was lining the pockets of the dirty ones, and how was Nick supposed to know who was clean? Hell, whoever the DA had been on the phone with in Mike's video sounded like law enforcement of some sort. They'd discussed rigging a trial and killing Mike like it happened all the time. They'd think nothing of ending Sasha and her daughter. Sure, Nick figured he could try the press, but he didn't have the kind of pull to get their attention, especially in a busy post-election season. *If* they ran with the story, it would be too little too late to save Sasha.

Raking a hand through his hair, Nick fixed his gaze on his woman again. What would life be without her? Could he live if the worst happened and he hadn't done *everything* possible to save her and Harper?

Fuck no. He was going to have to choose Plan *B*.

Turning the phone over in his hands, he sighed. Denial raged. Regret swelled. Fury decimated. *Son of a bitch*. He didn't want his vengeance to end this way. But he'd always put Sasha first. End of story.

Cursing, he looked up the number for the DA's office. After a little prowling, he found the man's direct line. Voice mail. Shit.

"Clifford, Nick Navarro here. Let's negotiate. I have what you want. I'll give it to you if you agree to leave Sasha Porter and her daughter alone. In exchange, you can have the video and my life. I will make sure she never says a word. That's the deal; take it or leave it. Be at Popp Bandstand at nine tonight."

Nick didn't tell the man to come alone; he wouldn't. Just like he also knew that Clifford would never believe that Sasha would keep her mouth shut simply because Nick had told her to. Men like Walter Clifford understood violence, brute force, and death. Luckily, Nick spoke his language. He probably wouldn't come out of this meeting still breathing…but neither would the fucker who had killed Mike and ruined Sasha's life.

As far as Nick was concerned, that was a fair exchange.

Feeling older than his thirty-three years, he stood, holstered his gun, and paced across the room to Sasha, bending to press a kiss on her forehead, his lips lingering. The inevitability of the moment choked him. He dragged in a rough breath filled with her floral scent and the smell of their sex. At least he'd be walking away with one of the best memories of his life. Better to go out on top.

"I'd hoped we'd have a million tomorrows, baby," he whispered. "At least I can give that to you and Harper. I love you."

Taking the car keys and weapon—leaving behind his phone, the video evidence, and his heart—Nick departed the motel and disappeared into the night.

* * * *

Sasha woke alone with a start. She sensed the emptiness in the room immediately. With a gasp, she sat up, looked around. Nick was gone, as was his gun. The phone and the computer still sat on the desk. What did that mean?

Heart pounding, she tossed on her clothes and searched the room, just in case. But as she suspected, Nick was nowhere in sight. She had an ominous feeling, a lot like the one she'd gotten the night Mike had disappeared.

She refused to lose another man she loved to the same killer. She would not lose Nick now that she'd started to live again.

What could she do? Where had he gone? How could she help him?

Sasha raced to his phone and looked at the last call he'd dialed. An unfamiliar but local number. She lifted the laptop lid to do a reverse search on the digits, but the open browser gave her the answer. Cold slithered through her blood. The DA's office. He'd located Clifford's direct line.

Why would Nick call the man? Sasha refused to believe he was selling her and Mike out. He wouldn't take favors from the criminal in exchange for the video. A few days ago, she might have believed the man was capable of that—and worse. Now she knew better.

She clicked on the other browser tab he'd opened. A local news story. Gasping, she read the headline. Josh had been killed in a seemingly random drive-by? Sasha didn't believe it had been happenstance for an instant. Clifford had offed his own employee before he could see Mike's evidence and take it to the task force.

Suddenly, she feared she knew exactly what Nick was up to.

Panic gripped her heart as she plucked up his phone and flipped through his contacts. Thankfully, there were few, and Xander was easy to find.

The man picked up on the first ring. "Thank fuck. After our last call,

I was afraid you were going to do something stupid and heroic, you prick. Don't—"

"I think he is," she breathed into the phone. "This is Sasha. I woke from a nap to find him gone. He took his gun and left his phone. The ADA we were going to see in thirty minutes is dead."

"Okay, don't panic. I talked to him maybe ten minutes ago. I'm hoping he hasn't been able to manage too much stupid in that time." Xander swore aloud. "Listen to me. Logan Edgington is one of my best friends."

"Former Navy SEAL. Nick told me."

"Yeah. He's headed your way. Best there is. Give me your location." As soon as she did, Xander went on. "I'll get him to you. I'm also trying to track Nick down. Any idea where he might have gone?"

Sasha tried to think but drew a blank. "It's a big city. He could be anywhere."

"Tell me the places you've been lately."

She recited each location in chronological order. "I can only think of one he'd go back to, and that's Popp Bandstand. It had meaning for him and Mike. On a Monday night, it wouldn't be that crowded, especially as the hour grows later. But he could be somewhere else entirely…"

"I'll keep working angles here. I need you to do something, Sasha. E-mail that video to every local TV station you can find. I'm doing the same in Lafayette. Tell them you're Mike's widow. We need to make Clifford a public target as quickly as possible. Logan can make the two-hour trip down there in about an hour and a half since he drives like a NASCAR pro. I'm also contacting the FBI. I tried to tell Nick that I know a guy, but he hung up. Sean will put us in touch with the right people." Xander finally took a breath. "We'll save Nick."

"I hope so." Sasha wished she could do more to help the man she loved since it felt as if sending videos to news outlets was something safe and removed. Something Nick would have wanted Xander to ask her to do. Like busy work.

"We will. He helped save me from doing something stupid and sacrificial when London was in danger once. I owe him."

"I can't lose him." She hated the tears in her voice. Now wasn't the time to fall apart.

"You've lost so much."

Yes. Losing Mike had wrenched her life apart. Losing Nick would forever rip her heart to shreds.

"Is Harper all right?"

"Great. Having fun. She's almost healed. Dr. Minn saw her this afternoon and was pleased with her progress. Remove her from your list of worries. We've got this."

"Thanks for everything."

"I'm texting you a picture of Logan, so you'll know the right guy when he comes to your motel door. Call me if you hear from Nick at all. I'll do the same."

With a murmured good-bye, Sasha hung up. If Logan was going to be here in just over an hour, she had some preparing to do. After sending the e-mails to all the TV stations, she grabbed a room key, darted out to the sporting goods store just down the street, and made one purchase, thanking goodness Louisiana had no waiting period.

Sasha was ready for whatever happened—except losing Nick. She was damn determined that wasn't going to happen.

Chapter Seven

Nine p.m. rolled around. Nick stood in the middle of Popp Bandstand, feeling the weight of his SIG in his hand. Any minute now, Clifford would show up with a squad of goons and shoot him.

But not before he put a bullet between the criminal DA's eyes first.

As if his thoughts conjured the crook up, Clifford strolled into the spill of light from the top of the dome accompanied by two thugs, one at each shoulder. It was still cold, so no one else occupied the park. No one would witness whatever happened next.

No one would see if Walter Clifford had him killed.

"Stay there," Nick insisted. "That's close enough."

"You don't tell me what to do, Navarro," the older man insisted. "Give me the evidence."

"You'll leave Sasha Porter and her daughter alone?" Nick hid his gun just behind his thigh, waiting for the right moment.

"Are you really that stupid? That bitch has seen whatever evidence her stupid lug of a husband dug up. She's a witness. A loose end. She needs to be six feet under. So does the kid. We don't need any more brats in foster care. I'll be doing the girl—and the state—a favor."

Nick gritted his teeth. Only one kind of man could kill a three-year-old. Talk about someone who needed to be six feet under... "Then I'm not giving you shit."

The DA laughed, the sound scratchy and mean. "That's fine. Dan?" He looked at the guy on his right. "Shoot the motherfucker. He should pay for raping my niece anyway. What a shame that he wanted revenge for his conviction so badly and drew his weapon on an elected official and two off-duty officers."

"Yes, sir. Between the pecs or between the eyes?" the cop asked.

"How about one of each for good measure?" Clifford gave Nick a smarmy smile of triumph. "Bye. I'll send your buddy's widow and her kid to be with you soon, too."

"You might want to hold up. I don't have the video with me, and if you shoot me now you'll never see it."

"I'll take that chance." The man looked at his cohort. "Do it now."

Dan raised his weapon and aimed. Nick hit the deck and rolled behind a pillar, his heart racing as he glanced around the column of stone and tried to line up for a clean shot at Clifford's head.

"Nobody move!" a different voice shouted into the chaos.

Nick froze. Who the hell had crashed their mutual murder party?

"FBI," that same voice called out. "Walter Clifford, you're under arrest for conspiracy to commit murder, solicitation of murder, tampering with evidence, and corruption. Hands up. Now!"

"Fuck you!" said the old man.

"You're surrounded," the federal agent warned.

Nick peeked around the column again. The FBI already had Dan and Clifford's other hired goon in cuffs. But the DA had raised his own weapon and pointed it at the nearest agent's head. "I'm not going down."

"You are, you bastard!" said a woman. Her familiar voice turned his veins to ice. "It's over."

Sasha?

Nick leapt to his feet and saw her emerge into a corner of the light with a big soldier-type he recognized as Xander's buddy Logan. Goddamn it. Why the hell had she come here and put herself in danger?

For him. Because she loved him. Because she refused to lose him. She'd risked herself, her future with her daughter, and all her precious tomorrows to save him.

Damn it, if Nick didn't love her even more. But he wished like hell she'd stayed at the scuzzy motel.

Clifford yanked the gun in her direction and aimed. "Die, bitch."

"No!" Nick shouted and leapt to his feet, gun ready, determined to somehow pull the trigger and end Clifford's miserable existence before he could fire Sasha's way.

To his shock, she raised a weapon of her own and pulled the trigger. Everyone froze as the report of gunfire rang in the air.

Clifford clutched his neck and staggered back. Blood spurted. He gurgled when he tried to breathe. Then he fell with a last gasp.

The FBI leapt to action to secure Clifford and surround Sasha.

Nick leapt over the railing of the bandstand and darted across the grass. "Sasha. Baby!"

She dropped the gun and fought her way from the cluster of agents to run toward him. "Nick! Oh my... I've been so worried."

The second he enveloped her in his arms, he gripped her tight, feeling her heartbeat, her warmth, her love. He was never letting this woman go.

"This nightmare is over, thank God. Where the hell did you get a gun?" he barked.

"I still have my Louisiana driver's license. I'd previously taken a gun safety class with my dad and passed. After you left the motel room, I woke and talked to Xander. Then I ran to the sporting goods store and bought this Baretta tonight. I wasn't going to sit around like a damsel in distress."

"But I wanted you to, damn it. Don't ever run off like that again," he chided.

"Then don't you ever run off on me, either. I'll never let you leave me behind to face life alone." She shook her head. "I'll always be by your side."

"But I wanted to save you, baby. That was my plan. That's why you came to me." He grabbed her arms. "You should have let me give you that much."

"At the expense of your life? You knew that was the likely outcome."

He hesitated, then nodded. "That's not important."

"It is to me! What I really need more than your protection is your strength, support, and love. We need to save each other."

She was right, and he couldn't have found a better woman for him if he'd searched the whole fucking planet. "I love you."

Nick saw the swarm of agents watching them. Reporters were beginning to appear around the perimeter of the scene, cameras rolling. He overheard swatches of their lead-in, talking about the leaked video and the warrant that had already been out for Clifford's arrest and speculating that Nick's conviction—among others—would likely be overturned.

"It is, and I'm so grateful. But you and I? We're just beginning."

"Yeah." Nick swallowed. "When you first knocked on my door, I only asked you to give me your body for four weeks. I'm thinking now that I need you to give me your heart for a lifetime."

She took his hand and faced the waiting agents. "You've got a deal."

Epilogue

Six months later

Nick smiled as he exited his truck and approached the blonde at the door who never failed to steal his breath.

"Well?" Sasha asked, toying with the sparkling pendant around her neck.

After she had wasted Walter Clifford, a slew of dirty cops, along with a few corrupt lawyers and a judge or two, had been exposed and convicted. Nick had insisted he and Sasha look forward together, not back. So he'd replaced the key Mike had sent her before his death with a diamond heart. He loved this woman, and he damn sure wanted her to remember that every moment of every day.

"You asking if I played nicely with the other boys and girls?" he teased as they headed into the house.

"Maybe I should ask if they played nicely with you." She thrust a hand on her curvaceous hip. "I still can't believe you wore that on your first day at S.I. Industries."

"What?" He looked down. A drawing of the Grim Reaper splashed across his chest with a caption that read *I Love My Job*. "This is my fancy T-shirt."

"Nick..." she chided softly.

"It is. And I did warn Javier and Xander that I wasn't a corporate guy. Besides, when they saw the shirt, they laughed."

She shook her head at him but her adoring smile was all he saw. "So...good day?"

"Yeah. S.I. Industries will always have security challenges. That reality goes hand in hand with technology and defense contracting. This job will be a challenge and I'm going to enjoy the hell out of it. I'm just glad my predecessor decided to retire." Nick felt sure the Santiago brothers had helped the man along with a fat paycheck, but since the guy had moved to Grand Cayman, Nick didn't feel too sorry for him.

"That's fantastic." Sasha hugged him. "I knew this would be the right career move for you."

"Totally," he assured. "Now, how about a kiss from my beautiful wife?"

A sweet pink crawled up her cheeks and her smiled turned come-hither as she sidled closer and stood on her tiptoes, eyes closed, lips parted. She didn't have to invite him twice.

Nick dove in and plundered her lips, dragging her against him with a groan so she could feel just how much he had missed her today.

"Hmm… How about more than a kiss from my beautiful wife?" he breathed against her lips.

She grinned. "I gave you a hot sendoff this morning."

"That was so twelve hours ago." He winked.

"You're insatiable…" She tried to sound chiding but her smug smile negated her tone.

"I prefer to think of myself as being too in love to get enough."

"Me, too," she whispered.

"Mommy." Harper came skipping into the room, baby doll in hand. "Daddy Nick!"

With a sigh of regret, Sasha gave him a last lingering peck then backed away just as Harper launched herself into his arms.

He caught the little imp and hugged her tight. "Hi, pumpkin. How was preschool today?"

"Fun." She hugged him tight. "Missed you."

"I missed you, too." He kissed the crown of her little blond curls.

"Hungry?" Sasha asked the girl.

"Yesth." She wriggled out of Nick's arms, distracted by her toys on the living room floor.

"Dinner will be ready in five minutes," Sasha told her daughter, then turned and made her way into the kitchen. "I need to set the table."

Watching the sway of her ass, Nick followed. "What smells so good?"

"Lasagna."

"Sounds scrumptious. Do I get dessert, too?" he asked suggestively.

His wife nodded. "Whatever you want, whenever you want."

"Be careful with that offer, baby." He nodded toward the breakfast nook. "That table looks awfully inviting."

Since he'd already fucked her sitting on, tied to, and bent over it more than once, Sasha flushed a deep red and cleared her throat. "Harper, go wash your hands before dinner."

"'K." The girl scampered down the hall.

Nick watched her go with a tug on his heart. The kid looked more like Mike every day, and he was so damn proud that he'd be raising Harper. He kind of thought his old buddy would be smiling down on them all, too.

"The final adoption papers came in the mail today," Sasha said quietly.

He turned back to her with relief. "So it's done?"

"Yes." She approached and took his hands, toying with the titanium band on his left ring finger. "She's officially Harper Navarro now. I told her that you would be her new daddy forever, and she was excited. My parents are thrilled. And I talked to Glen today. He understands and gave us his blessing. He also agreed to moving up here from New Orleans."

Nick let out a sigh of relief. "That's good. Mike's dad didn't have anyone left in New Orleans. We can take better care of him in Lafayette."

"Exactly. I've got calls into a few facilities around town. You know he'll want his own space, and he can still live semi-independently. It will be good for both him and Harper to spend more time together."

"Absolutely." And the man had been something like a father to Nick, too, so he was damn glad he'd be seeing more of Glen. "Thanks, baby."

"You had the idea. I just helped you follow through."

He sank his fingers into her hair and looked deep into her hazel eyes. This woman had haunted him, burned him with desire, and completed his heart in a way he'd never imagined. He was grateful every day that she had knocked on his door that cold November night. He felt incredibly blessed that Sasha had seen past his bluster, accepted his faults, and given him her heart.

"We make a great team, Mrs. Navarro," he murmured.

"We do. In fact, we're successful at just about everything we try."

"Yep. Moving a senior citizen won't be quite as gritty as finding hidden evidence, offing bad guys, and overturning my rape conviction, but I'm okay with slowing down."

"That's too bad because our lives will be significantly busier...in about seven months." Sasha took his hand in hers and placed it over her soft, still-flat belly.

Nick felt his heart stop. He couldn't breathe. He zipped his gaze to hers, delving for the truth. Love and joy radiated from her features. She fucking glowed.

"You're pregnant?"

She nodded. "I saw the doctor today. I didn't want to get your hopes up until I knew for sure, but it looks like I might have conceived just before the wedding."

Nick thought back, and he knew exactly when it had happened. That March night he had lured her to their backyard with a glass of wine and slowly seduced her under the moonlight had been more than special. At the time, it had felt monumental. Now he knew he'd been right.

Nick scooped her up in his arms and swung her around. "Ah, baby. I'm so thrilled. I told you that waiting-until-the-honeymoon thing was shit."

"You were right. I can't believe how happy I am." She hugged him tightly and curled her arms around his neck.

He gave her hair a gentle tug until their gazes fused. Nick felt their connection all the way down in his soul. "I'm damn happy, too. Let's stay this way, okay?"

"I'm planning on it." She slanted him a saucy stare, then glanced at the table. "So, after dinner...how about that dessert?"

* * * *

Also from 1001 Dark Nights and Shayla Black, discover Forever Wicked and Pure Wicked.

Sign up for the 1001 Dark Nights Newsletter
and be entered to win a Tiffany Key necklace.

There's a contest every month!

Go to www.1001DarkNights.com to subscribe.

As a bonus, all subscribers will receive a free
1001 Dark Nights story
The First Night
by Lexi Blake & M.J. Rose

Turn the page for a full list of the
1001 Dark Nights fabulous novellas...

Discover 1001 Dark Nights Collection Three

HIDDEN INK by Carrie Ann Ryan
A Montgomery Ink Novella

BLOOD ON THE BAYOU by Heather Graham
A Cafferty & Quinn Novella

SEARCHING FOR MINE by Jennifer Probst
A Searching For Novella

DANCE OF DESIRE by Christopher Rice

ROUGH RHYTHM by Tessa Bailey
A Made In Jersey Novella

DEVOTED by Lexi Blake
A Masters and Mercenaries Novella

Z by Larissa Ione
A Demonica Underworld Novella

FALLING UNDER YOU by Laurelin Paige
A Fixed Trilogy Novella

EASY FOR KEEPS by Kristen Proby
A Boudreaux Novella

UNCHAINED by Elisabeth Naughton
An Eternal Guardians Novella

HARD TO SERVE by Laura Kaye
A Hard Ink Novella

DRAGON FEVER by Donna Grant
A Dark Kings Novella

KAYDEN/SIMON by Alexandra Ivy/Laura Wright
A Bayou Heat Novella

STRUNG UP by Lorelei James
A Blacktop Cowboys® Novella

MIDNIGHT UNTAMED by Lara Adrian
A Midnight Breed Novella

TRICKED by Rebecca Zanetti
A Dark Protectors Novella

DIRTY WICKED by Shayla Black
A Wicked Lovers Novella

A SEDUCTIVE INVITATION by Lauren Blakely
A Seductive Nights New York Novella

SWEET SURRENDER by Liliana Hart
A MacKenzie Family Novella

About Shayla Black

Shayla Black is the *New York Times* and *USA Today* bestselling author of more than fifty novels. For over fifteen years, she's written contemporary, erotic, paranormal, and historical romances via traditional, independent, foreign, and audio publishers. Her books have sold millions of copies and been published in a dozen languages.

Raised an only child, Shayla occupied herself with lots of daydreaming, much to the chagrin of her teachers. In college, she found her love for reading and realized that she could have a career publishing the stories spinning in her imagination. Though she graduated with a degree in Marketing/Advertising and embarked on a stint in corporate America to pay the bills, her heart has always been with her characters. She's thrilled that she's been living her dream as a full-time author for the past eight years.

Shayla currently lives in North Texas with her wonderfully supportive husband, her teenage daughter, and a very spoiled cat. In her "free" time, she enjoys reality TV, reading, and listening to an eclectic blend of music.

Connect with me online:

Facebook: www.facebook.com/ShaylaBlackAuthor
Twitter: www.twitter.com/@shayla_black
Website: www.shaylablack.com
Instagram: https://instagram.com/ShaylaBlack/
YouTube: https://www.youtube.com/channel/UCFM7RZF38CqBlr6YG3a4mRQ

If you enjoyed this book, I would appreciate your help so others can enjoy it, too.

Recommend it. Please help other readers find this book by recommending it to friends, readers' groups, and discussion boards.

Review it. Authors need awesome readers like to you to tell other readers why you liked this book, so please review it at Amazon, Goodreads, or your favorite online bookstore. Nothing elaborate, just a few words. But it makes all the difference in the world.

Thank you so much for your support!

Discover More Shayla Black

Forever Wicked
A Wicked Lovers Novella
By Shayla Black

They had nothing in common but a desperate passion…

Billionaire Jason Denning lived life fast and hard in a world where anything could be bought and sold, even affection. But all that changed when he met "Greta," a beautiful stranger ready to explore her hidden desires. From a blue collar family, Gia Angelotti wore a badge, fought for right—and opened herself utterly to love him. Blindsided and falling hard, Jason does the first impulsive thing of his life and hustles her to the altar.

Until a second chance proved that forever could be theirs.

Then tragedy ripped Jason's new bride from his arms and out of his life. When he finds Gia again, he gives her a choice: spend the three weeks before their first anniversary with him or forfeit the money she receives from their marriage. Reluctantly, she agrees to once again put herself at his mercy and return to his bed. But having her right where he wants her is dangerous for Jason's peace of mind. No matter how hard he tries, he finds himself falling for her again. Will he learn to trust that their love is real before Gia leaves again for good?

* * * *

Pure Wicked
A Wicked Lovers Novella
By Shayla Black

During his decade as an international pop star, Jesse McCall has lived every day in the fast lane. A committed hedonist reveling in amazing highs, globetrotting, and nameless encounters, he refuses to think about his loneliness or empty future. Then tragedy strikes.

Shocked and grieving, he sheds his identity and walks away, searching for peace. Instead, he finds Bristol Reese, a no-nonsense beauty scraping to keep her business afloat while struggling with her own demons. He's intent on seducing her, but other than a pleasure-filled night, she's not interested in a player, especially after her boyfriend recently proposed to her sister. In order to claim Bristol, Jesse has to prove he's not the kind of man he's always been. But when she learns his identity and his past comes back to haunt him, how will he convince her that he's a changed man who wants nothing more than to make her his forever?

Holding on Tighter
Wicked Lovers, Book 12
By Shayla Black
Coming February 7, 2017

"Wait." Heath grabbed her arm.

Something electric arced between them, and she gritted her teeth against the sizzle.

The reaction made her even more prickly. "What?"

"Since we're off the clock and we've clearly set aside our working relationship for the moment, I think it's only right that I have the chance to say what I think of you."

She swallowed. If he was this hip to give her his opinion after she'd hurled a bunch of insults at him, she couldn't expect anything but ugly. Jolie sighed. It sucked but she'd earned it. "I'm listening."

"Excellent." He released her, his fingers curling into a fist as he began walking around her, studying her, drawing conclusions. "You don't trust men and that runs deep. It colors your decisions and prejudices everything you say to me. If you've never been in love, then your deep-seeded distrust must come from the lack of any stable father figure in your childhood."

"Thanks, Freud," she snapped.

Heath jerked back to face her and leaned in so close their noses nearly touched. "Am I wrong?"

She refused to stroll down that memory lane. "Does it matter?"

"I daresay it does. But we'll come back to that. If you were merely mistrustful of men, you would have waited until tomorrow and delivered a well-placed warning to keep me away from your sister. Instead, you came after me. And when you found me with another woman, your temper flared. If I merely lived up to your expectations of being a womanizing prick, that shouldn't make you angry at all, simply smug at being right. But you were livid. I doubt all that displeasure is on your sister's behalf. In fact, I suspect, Ms. Quinn, that you have more than a passing interest in me. You were jealous."

Apprehension raced through her veins. He was uncomfortably close to the truth. "You're egotistical."

"But I'm right." He gave her a tight smile. "For the record, if I intended to disregard policy and pursue a woman in the office, I wouldn't bother with your sister. As you say, she's naive and provides no challenge. But you . . . You would be far more interesting. Pretty, strong, smart, not easily bendable. Color me intrigued."

She tensed. "I'm your boss."

"Temporarily. We're both adults. Surely neither of us are prone to torrid emotional attachments. We could keep business separate from personal, couldn't we?"

Normally, she'd say yes. But working with him constantly buzzing around her, asking questions, and watching her every move had already dented her focus. "I have no intention of becoming your next conquest."

"Then it's good I never planned to pursue you."

Jolie wondered why, then dismissed the question as she buttoned her red coat. "Perfect. There's nothing left to say except I'm sorry for intruding on your evening. I hope we can forget this by morning."

She had to get out of here. She'd overplayed her hand and needed to regroup, to think about how to approach him tomorrow. The last thing she wanted was for Heath Powell to decide she was a challenge he intended to convert into his next bed partner. Normally, the sexual urges of a man wouldn't concern her unless she was interested. If so, she found a way to have him for a night or two, then ended it.

Something told her that nothing with Heath would ever be that simple.

But when Jolie turned her back on him and headed for the parking lot, he snaked an arm around her middle. "I never planned on pursuing you . . . but I've changed my mind."

Those soft words against her neck sent a shiver through her. "Get your hand off me."

"I'll bet the bitch act has scared off a man or two in your past."

She jerked away and cocked her hand on her hip. "Why is it that when a man is assertive, he's hailed as alpha and take-charge. But when a woman is equally assertive, she's a bitch?"

"Oh, let's be clear. I don't believe you're a bitch at all. I think that under your steely exterior is a woman with a soft heart. You take in stray employees the way other people foster animals. Their former employers have all cast them off. They aren't perfect but under your leadership, they're productive again. You make them work hard—as they should— but you're fair. You don't wheedle effectiveness out of them by pretending to be their friend. You tell them exactly what you expect. But you're chilly with me because you fear that if you don't guard against whatever I make you feel, I'll slip under your defenses and bruise that untried heart of yours."

God, he'd seen way too much of her. "Don't touch me again. If I want to be psychoanalyzed, I'll hire a shrink. Other than that, I expect you to be professional and do your job. You have my promise that I won't contact you after hours unless there's an emergency. Now we're done. Don't forget we have a staff meeting tomorrow morning at eight."

She pulled her keys free from her purse and walked away as quickly as her high heels could take her.

"I felt you trembling against me," he called after her.

Jolie clamped her lips shut. No sense in acknowledging that. The best way to handle a man like Heath Powell was to ignore him.

It took every bit of her will to follow her own advice. Why did he have to be right?

On behalf of 1001 Dark Nights,
Liz Berry and M.J. Rose would like to thank ~

Steve Berry
Doug Scofield
Kim Guidroz
Jillian Stein
InkSlinger PR
Dan Slater
Asha Hossain
Chris Graham
Pamela Jamison
Fedora Chen
Jessica Johns
Dylan Stockton
Richard Blake
BookTrib After Dark
The Dinner Party Show
and Simon Lipskar

Made in the USA
Columbia, SC
12 September 2017